THE FO...

*Follow the lives and loves of a complex family
with a rich history and deep ties
in the Lone Star State*

FORTUNE'S SECRET CHILDREN

*Six siblings discover they're actually part of
the notorious Fortune family and move to
Chatelaine, Texas, to claim their name...while
uncovering shocking truths and life-changing
surprises. Will their Fortunes turn—hopefully, for
the better?*

FORTUNE'S BABY SECRET

*After a devastating breakup, rancher Nash
Fortune hasn't been able to erase the stunning
Imani Porter from his mind. He's shocked when
he stumbles upon the oil heiress again—when
she's giving birth to his child! With only his
coldhearted dad as a model, Nash had sworn
off fatherhood forever. Can he overcome his
insecurities to be the parent his son Colt needs...
and, just maybe, the man Imani deserves?*

Dear Reader,

Thank you for choosing *A Fortune Thanksgiving*, a story that centers around my favorite holiday. There is something about that Thanksgiving that goes beyond gathering for good food to warm the heart and bring people together.

Both Imani and Nash became first-time parents, and it was so much fun having them experience that milestone together, sharing and overcoming many familiar fears that new parents face. Though Nash was doubtful about his ability to be a father to Colt, in time he grew to welcome his son into his heart and into his life with help from Imani. Imani had that strong family support and that independence but knew when it came to motherhood, she would need Nash's involvement.

But the best part of this story for me was watching Imani's and Nash's love for each other rekindle, sizzle, then blossom into something deeper and wonderful. The chemistry between these two people was off the charts, and it was fun to participate in this continuity with one of the hunky Fortune men.

I really hope you enjoy reading these characters' journey to love as much as I did. I would love to hear from you. Please consider joining my mailing list at michellelindorice.com.

Best,

Michelle

A FORTUNE
THANKSGIVING

MICHELLE LINDO-RICE

Harlequin

THE FORTUNES OF TEXAS

Special thanks and acknowledgment are given to
Michelle Lindo-Rice for her contribution to
The Fortunes of Texas: Fortune's Secret Children miniseries.

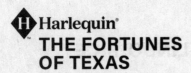

**THE FORTUNES
OF TEXAS**

Recycling programs
for this product may
not exist in your area.

ISBN-13: 978-1-335-99675-6

A Fortune Thanksgiving

 Harlequin Enterprises ULC
22 Adelaide St. West, 41st Floor
Toronto, Ontario M5H 4E3, Canada
www.Harlequin.com

Printed in Lithuania

MIX
Paper | Supporting
responsible forestry
FSC® C021394

Michelle Lindo-Rice is an Emma Award winner and a Vivian Award finalist. She enjoys reading and crafting fiction across genres. Originally from Jamaica, West Indies, she has earned degrees from New York University, SUNY at Stony Brook, Teachers College at Columbia University and Argosy University, and has been an educator for over twenty years.

She also writes inspirational stories as Zoey Marie Jackson. You can reach her online at www.michellelindorice.com or on Facebook.

Books by Michelle Lindo-Rice

The Fortunes of Texas: Fortune's Secret Children

A Fortune Thanksgiving

Harlequin Special Edition

The Valentine's Do-Over
A Beauty in the Beast

Seven Brides for Seven Brothers

Rivals at Love Creek
Cinderella's Last Stand
Twenty-Eight Dates

Visit the Author Profile page
at Harlequin.com for more titles.

For my husband, John, the man of my heart.

Thank you to my editor, Gail, who provided me with this opportunity to write for a continuity, and Susan for all your assistance along with the rest of the Harlequin team. Special thank you as well to my agent, Latoya, and my sister, Sobi.

Chapter One

If only she could stop shaking, Imani Porter could go through with this spontaneous wedding of convenience. She could recite the vows to a man she didn't love to give her son a father. A son scheduled to make his appearance really soon.

That's why as she stood under the awning of the justice of the peace in Stone Crest, Texas, clutching her bouquet of water lilies at the beginning of November, she reminded herself she was doing the right thing. Then, taking a deep, calming breath, Imani looked up into the face of her friend Simon Evans, who had proposed to her just seventy-two hours before.

The stand-in for a man who told her he didn't want to have children.

Imani had the best daddy in the world. Phillip Porter. Of course, she wanted the same for her son.

Her bridal ensemble included a designer wedding veil, a white one-shoulder jumpsuit with a cape and a wide skirt. And finally, she'd donned a pair of peau-de-soie pumps that pinched her toes. All because she knew Simon wanted them to look the part of a happy couple. For the pictures... *and* for her baby's sake. Even though they weren't actually a real couple, she suspected Simon very much desired that to be the case. She had met him during graduate school, when they were study partners, and they had remained loose acquaintances.

Until she learned she was pregnant a month after her relationship ended with the man of her dreams. During a bout of nausea at a nearby gas station, she had run into Simon, who had purchased her ginger ale and crackers. He had stayed with her until she felt well enough to drive. Simon became a shoulder, a sounding board, a support, which she appreciated. But he didn't make her heart race or her palms sweat like—

No. No. No. She couldn't allow herself to think about Nash Windham when she was about to promise a lifetime to another man. Squaring her shoulders, Imani slapped a wide smile on her face and tipped her head back to peer into Simon's blue-black eyes.

Her mother called them shifty eyes.

He reached over to take one of her brown hands in his fairer ones at the same time the judge entered the room. "Are you ready to become Mrs. Evans?" Simon asked, his voice smooth, like the bass guitar he strummed from time to time. Right as Simon asked the question, the baby kicked.

A sign that her child agreed?

She nodded, her lower lip trembling. The baby kicked again and she looked away. Wait…did her son disagree with her decision? Her heart began to pound and dread piled in her stomach. Maybe she was making a mistake by taking Simon up on his spontaneous proposal. Maybe she shouldn't have accepted his offer to be her baby's stepfather. Maybe she should have listened to her mother and grandmother when they advised her to have Simon sign a prenup.

After all, she had the means to be a single mom. At thirty-two, she was the proud owner of Lullababies, a high-end baby specialty store she had started with her cousin right after finishing design school. An accomplishment she was proud of.

Simon released her hand to greet the judge. She gripped the lilies she held and gave him a tight smile before drawing a few deep breaths. Seeing her purse on the desk, she battled the sudden urge to snatch it and flee. *You can't back out now.*

"Are you cold?" Simon asked, rubbing her shoulders, which made her teeth grit.

"N-no. I-I've just never been married before," she squeaked out, forcing herself to meet his eyes.

He chuckled and ran a hand over his goatee. "Neither have I."

The judge cleared his throat. "Are you ready to begin?"

With a jerky nod, Imani and Simon turned to face the magistrate. She shook so much that a couple of petals fell at her feet. The judge commenced using the traditional vows they had chosen. With a gulp, she slaked a glance at her groom, taking in his wide shoulders, powerful chin and smooth skin. Anywhere they went, Simon made the women take a second look, got them all hot and bothered, but she remained oddly…unaffected. Unmoved. Then, suddenly, another face, another body—tall and muscular with thick, dark hair and sultry amber eyes—popped into her mind, spiking her heart rate.

Clenching her jaw, she shook her head, shaking Nash out of her psyche. She didn't need the heart quivers. What she really needed was to think of the man she was about to marry today. This marriage would be a partnership.

Her mother, Abena, and paternal grandmother, Zuri, believed that Simon was marrying her because she was a Porter. He had his eye on a big payout—her grandfather's billion-dollar oil business in Cactus Grove. Hammond Porter, one of the only Black billionaires in Texas, had begun training her to lead his business from the time she was a child. Imani was his chosen heir and he planned to pitch her ascension to the executive board at Porter Oil. All of which Simon knew.

But Imani ignored her mother and grandmother's suspicions and their insinuations that he was a rebound. Because, in truth, she didn't view Simon through a romantic lens.

Then why are you marrying him? Zuri had asked her several times.

Because…

Imani allowed herself to get caught up, listening as Simon recited his vows with that warm baritone and surprising sincerity in his eyes.

They were going to be a happy family, with a happy life and an even happier baby. Weren't they?

"I promise to love, honor and obey…" he said.

Yep. She could do this.

Then Simon winked. A slow, suggestive wink.

That snapped her out of the fairy tale and back to reality. Panic weaved through her body at a rapid speed, tightening her chest. She took choppy breaths, fighting a sudden wave of nausea, of dizziness.

No. No. No. She couldn't do this. Her baby delivered two powerful kicks. Imani lifted a hand. "S-stop. We have to stop. Right now."

Imani dropped the flowers, then snagged Simon's attention.

"I feel like I'm about to pass out." Sweat drizzled down the side of her face. She could feel the curls wilting. Dang it. Her stylist had warned her against getting a blowout with the day so humid. She should have listened.

"Is it the baby?" Simon asked gruffly. He wrapped his

arm about her, his eyebrows furrowing into a deep *V.* She heard the judge calling for someone to bring her a glass of water.

Imani lifted a hand. "I just need…a second." She didn't have the heart to tell him that the thought of marrying him made her feel weak-kneed and sweaty—and not in a good way.

Simon scooped her close and led her over to sit on the judge's chair. She could faintly hear the judge asking for a medic. Her fiancé picked up a manila folder and pumped it back and forth, causing her curls to bob against her cheek. Next thing she knew, someone shoved a glass of water in her hand and commanded her to drink. As soon as she was finished, the paramedic on duty stuffed a thermometer in her mouth and wrapped her arm with a blood-pressure cuff.

"Is she going to be alright?" Simon asked, concern in his voice. Was he worried about the woman that she was, or about losing the perks of marrying an heiress? The fact that she didn't know the answer made her stomach bubble.

Oh, goodness. All this fuss made her face go hot, and the tighter the cuff got, the more embarrassed she became.

Simon was beside himself. "I hope this baby isn't trying to come today, of all days."

Was he for real? "What did you say?" she asked, enunciating slowly.

He stuttered, seeming to catch his faux pas. "I—I meant it's too soon. You're not due yet."

Of course, that's what he meant.

"Her blood pressure is elevated," the paramedic interjected, her voice steady. "But that's to be expected. A lot of brides get nervous." Peering down to look at her, the young woman asked, "Are you feeling contractions?"

"N-no. I'm only eight months pregnant so I've still got a few weeks to go. But my baby has been kicking up a storm."

"That's perfectly normal," she replied with a laugh, then patted Imani's arm. "I think your bride is safe to proceed. It's probably her nerves." The room cleared, leaving her alone with Simon.

More like Imani didn't want to get married. *Kick.*

And her baby didn't want her to do it, either.

Kick. Kick. Kick. "Alright, little one, I get it," she mumbled.

"What was that?" Simon asked, patting his brow. She couldn't look him in the eyes as he helped her to her feet.

"I'm sorry. I—I have to use the bathroom," she said, grabbing her purse and scuttling toward the door. Simon came toward her but she sped up and rushed into the hall. Imani hurried into the restroom so fast, she had to stop to catch her breath first before going into the largest stall. Once she was finished and had washed her hands, she dug into her purse for her sandals and changed out of her shoes.

She closed her eyes. Ah. What a relief. *You know what else would be a relief? Getting out of here.* Along with that thought came a sense of peace. And another kick from her little guy.

Decision made.

"Mommy hears you," she said. Quickly, she gathered her hair in a bun using a scrunchie from her purse, then opened the bathroom door and peered outside. Simon was a foot from the door. Waiting. Like a vulture with her as the intended prey.

"Are you okay?" he asked.

"No, but I will be." Imani raced down the hallway toward the exit with Simon following.

"*Don't do this!*" he yelled.

Imani waved a hand but didn't look back. "It's already done."

"If you walk through those doors. I'm done," he called out. "Lose my number."

She shrugged, unmoved by his idle threat, and sailed through the automatic doors. They opened with a swoosh and she ran out, grateful for the mild autumn day.

Imani beelined toward her Jeep Wrangler—a baby shower gift from Daddy—so glad she and Simon had arrived in separate vehicles. Simon had spent the morning at a spa—on her dime—while she had been at the hairstylist. Panting, she tried to stuff herself into the vehicle but the skirt was a pain. Good thing it was detachable. After snapping it off her waist, she tossed the flimsy material on the ground of the parking lot before settling inside the SUV. Imani took a moment to shut down her phone. Then, she pressed the gas, and peeled out of the lot.

A couple miles down the road, she slowed as a thought occurred. She couldn't go home. Simon might show up at her penthouse suite…accompanied by her mother and grandmother. She had planned to sublease her place since she would have been moving in with Simon temporarily while they searched for their permanent home. At his insistence. Simon felt she should purchase a more grandiose compound—again, his words—suitable for her elevated status as the next CEO of Porter Oil.

Abena and Zuri lived in Cactus Grove and had traveled to Stone Crest for the celebratory wedding brunch following her nuptials. The two women had been furious that a Porter would get married in a courthouse. But Simon had pressed her so hard to elope that she had caved, mollifying her family with the brunch.

Thank goodness she had insisted that Nia Okafur, her

cousin and business partner, not reschedule the meeting with a new artist and the textile vendor they used. Nia had flown to Paris to meet up with an artist who made one-of-a-kind baby blankets. Imani's cousin would be back in time for her delivery and would take over the helm of Lullababies while she was on maternity leave.

Her stomach growled. The little guy had gone quiet. Despite the pitiful situation of her own doing, she giggled and wiped her brow. Spotting a creamery, she veered into the long queue of the drive-thru lane.

So since her penthouse suite was out, where could she go? She had packed her weekender with comfy pjs and loungewear, intending to spend her first night as a new bride at Simon's place. That had put her on edge even though at eight months pregnant, they wouldn't have been consummating their union. They had agreed to a partnership. Or, as Simon called it, *a merger*.

Ugh. He really had been all about the dollar signs.

Jumping at the chance to marry the heiress of Porter Oil.

Maybe she could reach out to her brother, Jonathan... Naw. He was all the way in Dubai with her father. They had been building Porter Oil's legacy overseas for more than a decade. Imani didn't know how her mother tolerated such a long-distance relationship but whenever her parents reunited, they acted like randy teenagers.

Whatever. That wouldn't be her.

She supposed that was why she had run out on her own wedding. She wanted something more and she was at the place in her life where she went for what she wanted. And she'd start with a huge serving of ice cream—even though her stomach felt squirrelly all of a sudden—then she'd drive to one of the nearby towns and do some shopping.

Imani moved up a space in the queue.

She squirmed in her seat as guilt flowered in her chest. The magnitude of what she had done weighed on her shoulders. Oh my gosh. Even if he had ulterior motives, Simon hadn't deserved her running off like that. If only she had listened to Nia, who begged her not to take Simon up on his sudden offer of marriage. What had her cousin called it? *A pop-up proposal.*

The rocky road ice cream on display looked enticing, making her salivate. It also made her think of the first time she had met Nash Windham. The tears flowed easy—the result of guilt, missing Nash and pregnancy hormones. She struggled to speak clearly when it was finally her turn to order. By the time she got to the checkout window, Imani's body was shaking from her cry fest. She was the worst person in the world.

The young man at the window bent over to hand her the cone. She was sure her cheeks were red and puffy from crying. "Ma'am, are you okay?" he asked, his eyes widening with alarm when he saw her round tummy. He gave her a stack of napkins.

"Actually? No... I feel horrible," she sniffled, wiping her face and reaching out to take the ice-cream cone before handing him a crisp twenty-dollar bill. "Keep the ch-change. That's the least I can do." Before he could utter another word, she drove off.

A sharp pain sliced across her lower back—a sign she needed to calm down. Imani drew deep breaths, gripping the wheel with her free hand, and then began devouring her cone. Eating her feelings. Since being pregnant, food had become her go-to for every emotion she felt—joy, fear, loneliness and now guilt.

Feeling another cramp, Imani pulled over and finished her treat. Then she cleaned her mouth before blowing her nose. *Oh, no!* There was a huge chocolate stain across her bosom. She lifted the middle console to take out the small bottle of hand sanitizer. After squeezing out a tiny dollop, she rubbed her hands and then poured some on a napkin. She gently dabbed at the chocolate but her garment was probably ruined. Plus, she could feel a headache forming.

A fitting end to her disastrous non-nuptials.

Oh, well. She would change once she got to the strip mall. Imani shoved the image of her plush comforter atop her four-poster bed out of her mind and started up the vehicle, appreciating the gentle whir. Eyeing the phone in her bag, she bit her lower lip and decided to turn it on.

Sure enough, her phone pinged with multiple alerts. Two from her mom, one from her grandmother, five from Nia.

And one from Simon.

Ignoring the low-battery alert, she pulled up his text. We can still do this if you change your mind. Ugh. This man didn't know when to give up.

Their friendship had run its course.

She blocked him and deleted his contact information, then rubbed her lower back. Tossing her phone in her bag, Imani avoided her reflection in the rearview mirror. She couldn't face herself.

She couldn't face anyone.

Oh, Lord, she wasn't going to make it to the hospital. It was no use trying.

Parked on the side of the road, with no idea of her exact location, Imani wished someone would drive by. Anyone. Her phone had long died and she hadn't brought her charger with her that morning. She could see the cord on her coffee table and bit her lower lip to keep the panic at bay.

How many times had her mother and Simon told her to keep a spare in her car? If only she had listened…

After spending a few hours engaging in retail therapy, very much unaware that she was in labor, Imani had been on her way home late that evening when the first serious contraction hit. It only took a few minutes before she realized her multiple trips to the restroom could have been her water breaking. Somewhere on her journey back, her vehicle navigation system had lost signal and she had made a wrong turn. Now she was well and truly lost in these back roads. And now low on gas, with labor pains, she couldn't keep driving and put herself and her baby at risk. So here she was, in active labor with only the cows and a couple of goats for company.

Breathe, Imani. Breathe. In, out. In, out.

Oh, it was no use.

Her contractions were now coming so fast and furious, about a minute apart, that she struggled with remembering how to do anything she'd learned in Lamaze class.

I can't have this baby, out here in the middle of nowhere, alone.

But it looked like she might not have any choice in the matter. Her stomach muscles tensed, her body priming for another contraction. Holding on to the door handle and gripping her leather seat, Imani bunched her fists and screamed.

Chapter Two

As long as he lived, Nash Fortune would never forget the terror etched across Stanley Trotter's face after his new part-time employee had fallen off the horse at the Fortune Family Ranch. As foreman, Nash was responsible for the well-being of every single worker, and the fact that it had happened on his watch had left him shaken.

He headed out the front door of County General Hospital that Friday evening, having paid Stanley a visit. Thankfully, the other man had only suffered minor injuries and would be released in a couple of days before recuperating at home. He had been in good spirits, surrounded by his wife and baby girl.

Stanley had introduced Valentina and his six-month-old, Penelope, his voice filled with pride. Nash had felt a twist in his gut. One that felt oddly like jealousy. Nash had backed out of the room with haste, stating that he had to oversee the feed delivery for the cows, all the while grappling with that foreign yearning for family. Which was ridiculous. He had five siblings and they all lived in separate houses on the thirty-five-hundred-acre cattle ranch in Chatelaine Hills, purchased from a wealthy family who had relocated to Arizona. And since learning he was a Fortune a few months ago, Nash had inherited even more family.

Every time he thought about the entire Fortune clan welcoming him at his grandfather's bedside, his heart warmed. The bond between the Fortunes had made his decision easier to change his name from Windham to Fortune, though he would do anything to please his mom.

But he didn't have a wife. And he could have had one if he had allowed himself to fall for the only woman who had kept his interest past three weeks. *Imani Porter.* Just thinking about her made his insides quiver. He had met her outside an ice-cream shop when he lived in Cactus Grove, not too long after his father's death.

Their chemistry had been instant. With her smooth sepia skin, her generous lips and those ridiculous curves, Nash had wanted a taste of that more than the butter pecan in his hand.

Before he knew it, Nash and Imani were talking nonstop for hours and he had spent every free minute he had with her soaking in her sharp wit, her feisty spirit, her spunk. Nash remembered moments in bed where he would just watch her sleep, or stare into those dark chocolate orbs while she talked about her day. Just as Imani and Nash had reached the three-month mark, Nash's mother, Wendy, mentioned maybe it was time to start wedding planning.

Those words, spoken in jest, had scared him like nobody's business, but then when he broached the topic with Imani, expecting her to laugh along, she had grown serious and pinned that gaze on him. Like she had…*expectations.* Expectations of being a wife, a mother—she wanted five children, had even picked out names, he had learned. Expectations he hadn't shared. Nash had called it quits, though his heart had protested. And while he still missed that woman something fierce, Imani *was* the kind of woman someone settled down and started a family with. And Nash was doing none of that.

Nope. Not him.

His own father had pretty much cut him off, like he was one of his employees at Windham Plastics, and Nash had that man's blood in his veins. He couldn't chance messing up an innocent child's life, like Casper Windham had done to him. His father had been cold and distant all because neither Nash nor his siblings had been interested in working at the family business. He would never forget the disdain on Casper's face when they had expressed an interest in ranching.

"Ranching," Casper had yelled, "is beneath a Windham."

Nash had no idea how his parents had remained married for thirty-three years. He ran a hand through his hair and expelled Imani from his mind. The only reason he was even thinking about Imani and all of this was because of Stanley and his family.

Liar.

The truth was, that woman intruded in his thoughts more than he cared to admit. He had peeped her Instagram a few times, but Imani hadn't posted in months. In fact, her last post had been her dinner plate from their last date.

It had been a dinner they had shared because he hadn't liked what he had ordered. So she had given him some of hers. He had taken one last glimpse of their joined hands—his white, hers brown, resting at the edge of the table—and vowed to stay away from her Insta page.

Nash's new cowboy boots—a gift from his twin sister, Jade—crunched on the gravel as he made his way to his truck. The Lucchese Baron boots, made of cherry alligator-skin leather, cost about ten thousand dollars, and even though he was a Fortune, with more money than he could ever spend over centuries, Nash would never have bought himself a pair. He had to admit, though, that they kept his feet comfortable, especially after a long day at the ranch.

He toyed with the idea of manufacturing his own high-end boots with cork leather or some other alternative—and add to the many businesses the Fortunes had in the town—but he would tackle one business at a time, or hand off the idea to one of his siblings. Speaking of which, he had scheduled a family meeting on the eighth to discuss several ventures they were going into—the dairy farm, the petting zoo and fiber arts—where he planned to share his three-year strategic plan. Thankfully, his younger brother, Arlo, aka the ranch whisperer, was helping him look over the plans.

After jumping into his silver Range Rover, Nash put on Taylor Swift's "Back to December"—all Jade's fault—and began his trek home. His sister had dedicated that song to him when she heard about his breakup with Imani. She had done it as a spoof but the stupid song stayed in his mind and he tended to play it when he thought about Imani.

So, yeah, this had to be the thousandth time. Pitiful.

So many times, Nash had picked up his cell phone to call or had thought about paying Imani a visit, but he would keep telling himself he had made the right decision. She was better off without him and his messed-up genes.

Since it was a beautiful autumn evening, he decided to take the scenic route on the back roads and enjoy the colorful hues along the skyline. He had just finished the second replay of that darn song when he shot past a Jeep Wrangler pulled over on the other side of the road. It was angled so that its rear end jutted into the street. Adjusting his rear window, he peeked behind him. The hazard lights weren't even on. With the sun dipping low, that person was asking to get hit by a speeding truck or another passerby. A car shot by and honked its horn.

Nash didn't remember seeing anyone sitting in the driver's seat. Maybe the owner had had car trouble and left the car there. Yes, that made sense. He began to accelerate. But what if the driver was sick or something and he could have helped?

On impulse, he executed a U-turn and parked behind the vehicle, making sure he was a good distance from the curb. Nash hopped out of the Range Rover, went to his trunk to retrieve his jumper cables and then walked up toward the Jeep on the passenger side. He could hear a woman howling in pain and quickened his steps.

Tapping on the window, he yelled, "Do you need help?" making sure to keep both hands in sight. Because of the shadow, he couldn't make out the woman's face but he could hear her cries. She was sprawled across the back of the car. One leg was on the back headrest and other was on the floor. He averted his gaze.

"Y-yes," she called out, in distress.

Nash stiffened. *There was something about that voice...*

But then she said something that made Nash panic. "I'm in l-labor and it's t-too early," she said, hiccupping. "I was tr-trying to get to a h-hospital, b-but the baby is comi-i-in-ng." She dissolved into fresh tears. "I d-don't know wh-what to d-do." She tilted her head back and wailed. "My ph-phone d-died."

Nash had delivered a calf for the first time about three weeks ago, but he was ill-equipped to assist with bringing this woman's baby into the world. He yanked his cell phone out of his pocket, then called 9-1-1 and gave them his name, and a quick rundown of what was happening, turning his back to give the lady privacy.

He heard the clacking of keys before the operator said, "My name is Anna. The ambulance is on its way."

A loud groan came from behind him. "Hurry," he said, tamping down the sudden fear that he might actually have to deliver this baby out here in these back roads.

"I'll stay on the phone with you until the EMTs arrive. Can you tell me how far apart her contractions are?" Anna asked.

Nash opened the door and hunched his lanky frame inside, making sure not to bump his head. "How far apart are—" He felt his eyes go wide when he saw the woman, whose face was wet with perspiration. *"Imani?"* His mind raced.

Imani was here.

Imani was pregnant.

Imani was…*in labor*?

She lifted her head, her mouth popping open. "Nash? What are y-you—" A fresh contraction hit, cutting off her words. She closed her eyes and leaned deeper into the back seat. "I—I can't do this," she sobbed. Imani's eyebrows bunched together, and her lips pinched tight.

His heart hammered while his mind tried to grapple with what he was witnessing. Imani was pregnant…about to deliver a baby by the side of the road. How was any of this *real*?

"Sir? Hello? Are you there?" the voice on the phone asked. But all Nash could do was shake his head, his feet shackled to the ground. He was too overwhelmed to formulate words. To process what was happening.

Nash began to do the actual math in his head. *Is it possible that…? No, no, it couldn't be.*

"Help me-e-e-ee," Imani wailed, interrupting his flow of thoughts. "The baby is coming."

"Oh, God. The baby isn't waiting," he boomed into the phone, cupping his head with his free hand. "What do I do?"

"Okay, I'll walk you through all the steps but I need you to stay calm."

"Stay calm? Stay calm when a child is coming?" he yelled out. Imani was now crying. Seeing her body convulse alarmed him.

"Mom is already scared. You don't want her panicking," the operator said, the voice of reason. How could she sound so blasé when the most scary, miraculous thing was about to happen before his eyes? She urged him to inhale, exhale. Inhale, exhale.

To his surprise, that even, steady tone relaxed him. Somewhat. He followed her lead, then drew in a long, deep breath and squared his shoulders. "Okay. Okay. I'll try."

"Good—now, do you have a blanket or anything?"

Blanket! "Y-yes, I've got one in the back of my truck."

"Great, go get it. Put the phone on Speaker so Mom can hear while you go get the blanket."

"I'll be right back," he said, doing as the operator asked.

"N-no, don't leave me again," Imani begged, eyes welling.

That face gutted his heart. "I'm not leaving you," he assured her quietly, "I'm just getting a blanket." She pierced him with a gaze before giving him a jerky nod. He dashed to get it, his heart thumping along the way.

He returned in time hear her scream. Oh, Lord, if she kept crying like that, he was going to fall apart. He couldn't stand her being in pain.

"Owww," Imani moaned, then panted, her eyes closed, her head moving back and forth. "I've got to push."

"I know you do," the operator said. "But I'll tell you when."

Nash swallowed and cleared his throat. He could hear the faint sounds of the ambulance but there was no telling how far away it was. Anna directed Nash to place the blanket under her legs—which was a monumental feat between contractions—and then he was holding one of her hands. Well, more like she was squeezing his hand like it was a sponge, while he was yelling at her to push.

The ambulance in the distance was getting louder and louder. Closer and closer.

"Push, Imani! That's it. That's it. You got this."

She released his hand and gripped the edge of the seat. Finally, after one final strong grunt, a baby boy entered the world.

In his hands.

Whoa.

Body shaking, this time with a mingling of laughter and tears, Imani stretched her hands toward Nash. He placed the precious package in her arms, through his own wall of tears, while she hugged and kissed her baby. Somehow, Nash remembered to record the moment and snapped a picture of Imani and the newborn.

He heard the operator asking if the newborn had cried, but then the EMTs arrived and worked on clamping the umbilical cord. Nash fought back more tears when they extended the offer to him to cut the cord. What an honor.

Moving quickly, they wrapped the baby in a blanket. Then Imani's son opened his mouth and let out a piercing bellow.

The EMT worker was about to hand Imani the baby, but she gestured for him to give her son to Nash and asked for his phone.

Squaring his shoulders, he scooped the infant that already had a hold on his heart close to his chest. The emotional weight of the moment was his undoing. He could hear Imani's sniffles as his gaze pinned on the tiny curious eyes looking back at him, as he took in the fingers, the toes, *the perfection*. He patted the small head filled with light brown curls.

The next thing Nash knew, the baby was being gently extricated out of his tight grasp by the EMT, who was telling him they needed to get mother and child to the hospital. He registered the other paramedic helping Imani out of the rear of the Jeep and rushed to assist. She tossed Nash his phone, then yelled for him to grab two bags out of her trunk and to get her keys out of the ignition. One was a baby bag, she said, and one was her "motherhood" satchel, which she had kept stowed there. There were also a couple shopping bags and a huge weekender that she said she didn't need.

Right before they placed her on the gurney, Imani gripped his hand. He snatched her close, needing the connection. She snuggled into him as they embraced, rocking back and forth, crying tears of joy and relief.

"You did good," he whispered, then took a picture of Imani and the baby, even as he heard the EMTs saying once more that they had to get to the hospital.

Imani nodded, then cupped his head and whispered, "And, you just delivered your son."

Chapter Three

Rarely was he ever without words. But when Imani whispered that sentiment to him, confirming what he'd known in heart to be true, Nash lost his breath.

He had a son.

One whom he had helped find his way into this world.

And his life would never be the same.

That stunning revelation buzzed around his mind as he watched the ambulance depart. Without him. He kept his eyes peeled until the vehicle was out of sight. Nash ached to get over to the hospital, but he knew he couldn't leave without securing Imani's vehicle. Rushing into action, he called for a tow truck. He'd have them drop the Jeep at his place for now.

All throughout the call, he thought of Imani's face as the ambulance doors closed. She had those brown eyes trained on him, their child in her arms. She had waved, like she was saying goodbye, like she had no expectations she would see him again.

His gut twisted. Was that what Imani wanted? Why she had kept her pregnancy a secret from him? To raise her child alone? As soon as the thought occurred, he chastised himself. She was probably honoring his wishes. Imani was an independent, proud woman and his desire never to be a father had created the rift between them that had ended their relationship. Of course, she wouldn't reach out.

Though he understood her reasoning, his heart hurt and his conscience churned.

How could he have known that the few seconds of holding such precious cargo would cause such a life-altering shift?

Regret whipped at him. He had missed seeing Imani's tummy grow round with their child. Had missed hospital visits—seeing his son's development in the womb, hearing his heartbeat. He gripped the back of his head and bunched his lips as he faced the knowledge that he could never get those moments back.

What if he hadn't driven this path this evening? He released a guttural groan. Would he have ever known? Would she have ever told him?

He could have gone on with his life, unaware, while there would have been a child yearning for him. A child with a cavity in his heart because of an absentee father. Nash clenched his fists. He couldn't let that happen.

But did he have the skills? That fear gnawed at him. Casper Windham hadn't. It wasn't far-fetched to believe Nash didn't, either.

Maybe he should stay far away from Imani.

Then his thoughts flip-flopped. But his son's piercing eyes served as a siren for his soul. Nash couldn't keep his distance just yet. He would at least check on the baby and Imani at the hospital.

Nash placed another call, this time to his brother Arlo, who answered on the second ring. "Hey, bro. Something came up—" *Something came up?* How distinctly vague. It was more like a meteorite had crashed into his life, obliterating his status quo. But mentally, he wasn't at the place where he could share the truth just yet. Nash snaked a hand through his hair. "I won't make it back to the ranch in time for the feed delivery. Miss Phyllis said she would call the ranch office when it was on its way. Do you think you can cover for me?"

"Yeah, right." Arlo snorted. "You just don't want to deal with Miss Phyllis. Everybody knows she's sweet on you."

Picturing the older woman with poufy blond hair that they believed to be in her seventies, and who ran the register at the Longhorn Feed Store, Nash gave a little laugh. "Stop it. She messes with everybody that goes in there. Not just me."

"Yeah, but you're the one she says has the—" his voice took on a high pitch "—movie star looks."

This was what he didn't like about having siblings. A little extra attention from an older, slightly eccentric woman was fodder for some good old-fashioned ribbing.

Nash rolled his eyes, then said, "No, this has nothing to do with Miss Phyllis" in a much more serious tone.

"Wait... Are you okay?"

The concern in his brother's voice threatened to snap the small thread of his control. "I hope to be," Nash answered, his tone grave.

The line was quiet for a second. Nash imagined his brother was telling himself not to pry. After a beat, Arlo cleared his throat and said, "I'll take care of the feed. Handle your business and I'm here if you need."

"Thank you." As soon as the call ended, the tow truck came. Once he had Imani's vehicle squared away, he jumped in his SUV to make his way back to the hospital. The trip had his heart pounding just like before, but this time the reason was much more palpable.

He was on his way to see his child.

Surreal.

That knowledge made him grip the wheel tightly. Nash used the voice-calling app and got his mother on the phone. Since she currently lived alone, he and his siblings made a point of calling or visiting with her once a week. But today wouldn't be just a random conversation. Today, he was reaching out because he had a dire need.

Wendy answered, sounding oddly cheerful, more than she had been in months. Normally, he would have questioned his mother about her uncharacteristically chipper behavior, but she didn't give him an opening to respond as she yammered on about some sewing or knitting something special. He wasn't processing all she was saying, but to be fair, but he had big news filling his brain.

"Mom." She kept talking.

A little louder. *"Mom."* She still didn't hear him. Nash interrupted Wendy in midsentence with a firmer tone, to drop his news bomb. "Mom, I just delivered my baby."

A harsh intake of breath. Then silence for a beat before she breathed out, "Say what?"

"You heard right. I have a son," he croaked out, grappling with the unbelievability of those words. As of less than an hour ago, Nash was living a new reality.

"Son, if you're pulling my leg right now, this isn't funny."

"I'm not joking."

"You mean I'm a grandmother again?" she boomed. Oh, she was definitely listening to him now. Nash used the button on his steering wheel to lower the volume. "This is one hot season for my kids falling in love, having babies or finding babies."

She sure was right. One of his younger sisters, Sabrina, was now five months pregnant with twins she called Peach and Plum, and Ridge had indeed found a three-month-old baby, Evie, in a haystack, right along with her mother, whom Ridge called Hope since she didn't remember who she was. Nash could hardly keep up.

"Nash, did you hear me?" Wendy asked.

"I'm sorry, Mom. Did you say something?"

"I asked if you'd fill in details for me, son. Like, who is this mystery woman? And did you know about the pregnancy?"

"It's Imani." He waited for that bit of news to settle.

"*Imani?*" she screeched a few seconds later. "As in Imani Porter? Man, you're just laying it on me, right now. You know how much I loved Imani. I thought she was perfect for you. Remember?" Her voice escalated as she rattled on. "Wait. She's here in Chatelaine? What's she doing all the way out here? Hang on—did she move here from Cactus Grove? What are the odds? But what about her company? Oh, my goodness. Imani!"

Nash lifted a hand even though his mother wouldn't be able to see his gesture. "Mom, you have to slow down so I can answer even one of your questions," he chuckled.

"Oh. Okay…good point. You caught me off guard. Whew, let me take a sip of this lemonade and then I'll let you talk."

"Sounds good." When Nash heard a refreshing sigh, he smiled and began. "I was on my way back from the hospital after checking in on Stanley, when I decided to take the back roads. And I spotted this Jeep on the side of the road at an odd angle. I don't know why but something made me turn around, and I'm glad I did because there was this woman hollering that she was in labor. So I called 9-1-1 and when I stuck my head inside, I saw Imani. *Imani.*" Even talking about it aloud, Nash still couldn't believe it. "The funny thing is, she had been pressed on my mind and the next thing I knew, I was helping her deliver our child. My son."

"Wow... Just wow." She didn't say anything for several beats. "Imagine that." The fact that his mom appeared awed and at a loss for words was rare.

"Yeah, with everything going on, I didn't get a chance to ask her any questions, like what she was doing here." A thought struck. "Unless she was on her way to find me?" Hope sprung wide like a flower in bloom. Maybe Imani had intended to tell him that she was having his child, but had gone into labor along the way.

"Whatever the reason, you were meant to be there at that precise time," his mother said. "You were meant to see your child enter this world, and you're destined to be in his life. What's his name?"

The fact that he had no idea made Nash once again question his place in his offspring's life. "I don't know, Mom."

"Oh."

Inadequacy lashed his heart. What kind of father didn't ask the basic question, like his child's name?

"With everything going on, I didn't think to ask. I was just relieved that Imani was alright and that little man was crying— Man, do his lungs work..."

"Don't go reading anything into that," Wendy cautioned. Dang, his mother was a mind reader. As usual. She continued, "For all you know, Imani may not have picked out a name yet. I know Casper and I had no idea what to call baby number six. I still don't know how we came up with Ridge, but it fits."

When he remained quiet, she added, "Shake it off, son. It sounds as if this baby made a surprise appearance. What matters is that he's healthy."

Trust his mom to defend his oversight and offer up a rational excuse. Nash swerved off the road and onto the curb. He cupped his head and admitted, "I don't know if I can do this, Mom. I don't know if I can be a father. It's not like I had an exemplary role model."

"Son, you can and you have to. You're too hard on yourself and I blame Casper for that. Nothing you did was good enough. You don't even see your awesome accomplishment today. Lots of new fathers pass out or lose control during childbirth. Your own father threw up in the delivery room when you and Jade were born. I applaud you for your courage and for being there when Imani needed you most."

His lips quirked as he pulled back onto the road. "This is the first I'm hearing that about my father." He refused to refer to Casper as *Dad* anymore.

"Well, Casper was a proud man and he was all about appearances. He felt showing weakness was unmanly. Which was plain dumb. No nicer way to say that." His mother released a long plume of air. He could imagine her pacing back and forth as she emphasized her point. "Look, I know your father did his share of damage but you are one-half me as well and I'd like to think I was a good mother."

"Not just *good*, Mom. You were—are—the best. You singlehandedly raised six of us, practically on your own. We are all thriving because of you."

"Oh, thank you for that." Her voice hitched. "Someday in the future, your child will say the same about you. Trust me on that."

Wendy's quiet certainty pierced through his doubts, and he exhaled. "Okay, Mom. I'll start by establishing visitation with Imani and I'll put in an ad for a nanny—"

"No. No, nanny, son. You need to be hands-on," Wendy insisted. "How else are you going to know for sure if fatherhood is for you?"

"Okay, Mom. I will do my best."

That was the best response he could give without lying to his mom. Nash wasn't as convinced as Wendy seemed to be in his potential parenting skills. The fact was that he was a product of Casper Windham as well—an absentee father—which couldn't be so easily discounted.

"Have you told your sisters and brothers yet?" Wendy asked, once again jutting into his thoughts.

"Not yet. I'm very much still trying to wrap my mind around all this."

"This is not the time to isolate yourself, son," his mother warned. "This is the time to embrace us, to allow us to be your strength and to celebrate with you."

Nash relaxed his shoulders and leaned back into the seat. "Once again, you're right, Mom. This is why I had to talk to you first. You help me get my head right. As soon as I've visited with Imani, I'll let everyone know."

"Alright. I'll await your call to come see my grandchild."

"You got it."

After hanging up, Nash turned into the parking lot of the hospital and scanned the lot for a spot. He found one near the entrance and pulled in. Somewhere in that building was the mother of his son and his child.

That knowledge humbled and grounded him. Nash opened the door and ventured out, then strolled across the lot. Snapping his fingers, he decided to make a stop at the gift shop. There was no way he was going to enter that hospital room with Imani and his future heir empty-handed. After all, he was a Fortune now, and so was his son—he hoped to give his progeny his last name—and what was the point in having money if he didn't splurge when it counted?

But as it turns out, his last name had drawn a small group of onlookers including the press. Well, *press* was too generous a word for the two reporters in their town. He had provided his name to the 9-1-1 operator and somehow, the staff at *The Chatelaine Daily News* must have learned that Nash Fortune had helped a pregnant woman and were labeling him a hero. Ever since Sabrina talked him into plastering his face on that billboard across from the GreatStore in town as the face of the Fortune Family Ranch, he couldn't do anything without being recognized.

It was a daggone nuisance.

The reporters peppered Nash with questions—this was definitely juicier than cattle ranching—but he declined to provide a statement and made his way to the gift shop. However, they got their money shot of him carrying an oversize teddy bear and a gift basket.

Great. That picture would be front-page news in Chatelaine Hills. Thank goodness, they didn't know it was his son. *Yet.* When the elevator doors closed, Nash knew he had to get ahead of the gossip mill. The last thing he wanted was for his siblings to learn about the newest addition to the family from anybody but him. Nash sent a text to the group chat.

Guess who became a father today?

Then he shut down his phone.

Chapter Four

Seeing Nash Windham hold his son in those strong arms was branded in her brain for life. What a story to tell their baby boy one day.

Telling Nash about his becoming a father was something she should have, *would* have, done if she had to do it all over again. Regardless of how he felt about fatherhood. The look of wonder and confusion on his face tore at her conscience.

No man should learn of his parentage that way.

It had been a shock for her when she first discovered she was pregnant, but she had *months* to get used to the realization that her life would change. Nash didn't have that luxury.

Snuggled under the plush comforter—a baby-shower gift handknit by her grandma—in her hospital room at County General Hospital, holding her son against her, Imani inhaled. Enjoyed the newborn baby smell, the feel of his soft skin and his small sighs as he slept in her arms. She released a breath of air and smiled. Nash should be here with her, sharing in the miracle of their child, equally enamored by the act of him simply breathing.

Imani had been researching the birthing process when she stumbled upon the fact that Black mothers and infants had a higher mortality rate than other populations in the US. That knowledge had left her shaken. And scared. Plus, going into labor in a deserted area had drastically reduced her chances of survival. So to have Nash show up when he did was an act of divine providence.

And for her, proof that Nash was meant to be a parent, even if he didn't believe he should be. That had been the actual topic of their last conversation as a couple. His feeling ill-equipped to be a husband or a father. Imani had disagreed, having gotten to know the caring, thoughtful man who was Nash Windham. Though they had been together for just three months, they had developed strong feelings for each other—okay, might as well call it *love* on her part—but Nash's fear had superseded everything else. He had been so vehement in his objections that she hadn't fought their inevitable parting.

Hadn't wrangled for her child to have his rightful father in his life.

Instead, mere hours ago, she had been about to give her son a replacement father. Imani wiped the sudden tears in her eyes from the guilt of keeping silent.

She had embraced impending motherhood—the all-day morning sickness, the sonograms, the Lamaze class, the gag-inducing glucose test. All of it. In fact, she'd *welcomed* it. Even the labor had been worth it. She touched the baby's nose, unable to suppress her smile. Because look at the outcome. Her heart expanded.

But now, she knew how wrong she was.

And how right Abena had been, when her mother beseeched her to tell Nash the truth. Maybe it was time she started listening to her mother and grandmother. She could hear their voices, cautioning her not to spoil the baby by keeping him in her arms. With a sigh, Imani rested the sleeping infant in the nearby bassinet.

Immediately, she fought the urge to pick him up. At seven pounds, nineteen inches, he looked so tiny, so…alone, in that plastic container, squirming, trying to get comfortable. Plus, his little cap was coming off. There was a card taped to the exterior with his birth weight, height and name written in permanent black marker.

Imani blinked back tears. Her little pumpkin's lower lip was trembling. One little foot stuck out from under the blanket. The thin receiving blanket, lined in pink and blue, must not be warm enough. She rushed over to retrieve a thicker blanket out of her baby bag to drape across his body.

Just as she was finished, the nurse entered the room. Heading straight for the sink to wash her hands, she murmured, "I'm back to check on you and baby. How are we doing?"

"It's going good so far," Imani said. "Thank you for the use of your charger. I'll call my family soon." As soon as the phone juiced up—there had been countless pings and voicemail message alerts. She had placed her phone on Silent while she cared for her baby.

"Wonderful. And you're welcome. It's good to get folks to rally around you and share your good news." There was the unspoken question of where the boy's father was, but the woman was too polite to ask.

Imani was feeling lonely but she was waiting to see if Nash showed up. She wanted them to have private bonding time before notifying her family. But it had been over an hour and he wasn't here yet… Nevertheless, she kept her tone confident, as she could see the older woman was concerned about her.

The nurse removed the thick blanket and placed it on

the side of the bassinet. "Let's not do a thicker blanket," she said in a cautioning, matter-of-fact tone. "We don't want the baby to get too warm. Overheating can increase the risk of SIDS."

Imani's eyes went wide and her heart thundered in her chest. "I didn't know that," she breathed out, wrapping her arms about her. Motherhood was scary, much scarier than she imagined. How was she going to raise her child alone?

"That's why we're here. To help you," the nurse offered, giving her a kind smile. She then rewrapped him tight, like a butterball, before grabbing the handlebar.

"Are you taking him again?" she asked, eyes pinned on her son. She didn't want to him out of her presence, especially after that warning. Upon arrival, they had whisked the infant away to the NICU to check his oxygen levels and his body temperature before bringing him back clean, swaddled and crying at the top of his lungs. Then they had placed the tag around her hand and his ankle.

The minute she held him, he had ceased. Wow. The wonder of being his favorite person had flooded her with joy. Imani cherished the skin-to-skin contact, falling in love with him even more with each passing minute.

"No. I'm here to check in on you to find out how the nursing is going," she said. "He's at a good weight at seven pounds, but we want to make sure he's getting the nutrients he needs. The lactation specialist told me you had a good session."

Imani relaxed. "I got him to latch on like you showed me, but I don't know how much he actually ate. But he burped." She couldn't hold her proud smile.

The nurse beamed. "Don't worry. He's getting something. The first few days you're producing colostrum, which is all he needs." She smiled. "Did he get a diaper change?"

"Oh, boy, did he." Imani chuckled. "I had to put on a new onesie."

"Great. It sounds like you're doing well. Remember, you can always hit the Call button if you need any help at all." Imani nodded but she was hoping not to have to do that. When she went home, she would be on her own. Might as well begin now. "Can I get you some yogurt and fruit?" the nurse asked.

"Yes, that would great. Thank you."

At that moment, Nash entered the room. Imani's heart leaped at the sight of him. She knew her face reflected how she felt. Nash gave her a hesitant smile. He was holding an oversize teddy bear and a gift basket with an assortment of chocolates. "Hello. I hope it's okay that I'm here."

"I'm glad to see you," she breathed out, dabbing at her eyes. He placed the gifts on the ledge near the window. He wiped his palms on his pants and stood waiting.

Awkward. She couldn't think of a single thing to say.

"Oh, is this Dad?" the nurse interjected, looking between them. Imani could see the relief in the other woman's eyes. She could also see the slight panic in Nash's, but he was waiting for her to respond.

"Y-yes, it is," Imani answered, licking her suddenly dry lips. Nash squared his shoulders and slid his glance over to the baby. "You can hold him," she offered, "but you have to wash your hands first." She chided herself for being so nervous around Nash. After all, he had seen her at her most intimate state.

Nash cleansed his hands and then took a tentative step toward the bassinet, then another, before closing the distance. He held on to the sides, his chin dipped to his chest and he just stared down at his son.

"I'll be back in a minute to get you tagged so you can

see the baby anytime," the nurse said, giving a wave before leaving the room.

Nash's eyebrows rose. "His name is Colt." He shot her a glance, his eyes wet, his voice filled with genuine astonishment. "You remembered."

"Y-yes. I remember everything about us." Imani sniffled. This reaction couldn't be blamed on her hormones. She had written in *Colt Windham* on the card, a bold move, but she hadn't known if Nash would get it. Would appreciate the significance.

"So do I." His look of tenderness made her stomach knot. The air thickened between them, unspoken feelings lurking under the depths of their gazes. But she held contact. She wouldn't back away from the memories.

One night wrapped in each other's arms, somehow, their conversation had veered toward favorite names. She believed the topic was, if you could name yourself, what would it be...or something like that. Imani shared how she loved the name Olivia. And that's when Nash told her about his love for horses. He'd had pictures all over the walls in his room when he was a boy. Nash had asked his parents for a male horse for his birthday, as well as a cowboy hat and boots. He had proudly declared that he planned to name his horse Colt. Casper had yelled at his six-year-old son that getting a horse was a dumb idea and spewed that the name he had chosen was even stupider, and snarled, "If you're going to name a horse, give it a strong, solid name."

Nash had admitted to her he'd cried and cried, and though his mother consoled him, telling him that it was a lovely name, he had been heartbroken. His father had refused to give him the one thing he desired most—to be around horses. Casper had bought him LEGOs instead—something plastic. Like the family's plastic business.

Imani's heart had hurt for that little boy. She had heard the anger in Nash's voice as he recollected that painful memory. So she hoped that Nash would see her gesture for what it was—an invitation for him to be in Colt's life. An acceptance of a name Nash had chosen.

"What do you think of my calling him Colt?" she whispered.

"I think it's a wonderful name," he choked out. Then he admitted in a low voice, "Do you know even though I own several horses—Midnight, Onyx and Leviathan—I have never used that name?" He shook his head. "Wow."

"It's a strong name." Blinded by her tears, Imani had to grab a few tissues to compose herself.

Nash bent over and picked up the baby in his arms. "Hello, Colt." He sat on the bed next to her and they both watched the sleeping child.

At that moment, Colt sighed. Like he was content. Then he smiled. Like all was right with his world because he was in his father's arms.

Imani was so overcome, her shoulders shook as she quietly wept.

Nash touched her face briefly. "You have given me a gift I didn't know I wanted. I promise I will do my best to be a good father for Colt." He cocked his head. "I know you have a business back in Cactus Grove, but I would love it if you considered staying here in Chatelaine Hills for a while? I have a two-bedroom guesthouse behind my house on the ranch and we could raise our son together. Well, it's actually an old carriage house that the previous owners converted." Before she could respond, he added, "You don't have to answer now, just please think about it." His expression was earnest, almost like he was pleading his case, as if she needed any convincing. She wasn't about to deny her son this opportunity to have his father in his life—and she hoped this experience changed Nash's mind about fatherhood. Plus, she needed a place to hide out from her nonwedding drama.

It was a win-win.

"I don't need to think about it. I know in my heart it's what Colt needs. How about I stay for about four months?"

His eyes brightened. "That's way more generous than I thought you would give."

She rested her head against Nash's chest. "I'm looking forward to this time with you." She wouldn't mind *forever*, but she would take what he could give. For now.

Nash placed Colt back in his bassinet, gently resting him on his back.

"There's one more thing you should know. Two, actually." He tapped his chin. "No, make that three."

"Okay." She squared her shoulders, bracing herself for what he was about to lay on her.

"First, I changed my surname. I'm Fortune now. Nash Fortune."

Her eyebrows rose. "Whoa. I'd love to hear the backstory."

"I'll catch you up," he said with a wave. "Just know, for me, this name change was a new beginning. A fresh start. So I'd love for our son to also carry this name."

"Yes." Her heart expanded. "It's an easy fix as I didn't complete the official birth-certificate papers yet." She peered at him from under her lashes. "I was hoping we both would sign."

He gave a jerky nod, stuffing his hands in his pockets.

Imani could see Nash still had some qualms, which was to be expected, but she was glad he was taking the right steps for his child. She cleared her throat. "So what's the other two?"

"Huh?"

"The other two things you had to say," she persisted.

"Oh." He raked a hand through his hair. "I think our baby announcement is going to be front-page news, and I wanted you to be prepared. We might have reporters waiting outside when we leave the hospital."

She pursed her lips and teased, "So you're a celebrity now."

Nash rolled his eyes. "It was Sabrina's idea to slap my face on a billboard in town and I regret it."

"I did tell you when we first met that I thought you were a model."

"Please. Don't remind me." He exhaled. "And number three is that I've alerted my family about the baby. And if I know them, they are going to invade this space. I don't know if you're up to all that but I've held them off until tomorrow."

"Bring it on," Imani said. "It feels great to know my son is going to have a huge extended family." That made her think of her loved ones. "Speaking of family, can you pass me my phone? I'm pretty sure my mother is worried sick about me, and she'll want to meet her grandson. Plus, I've got to let my dad know he's a grandpa."

"I'm going to go check out the guesthouse, make sure everything is in order," Nash said, after handing her the device. She sensed it was more to give her a private moment with her relatives, which she appreciated. "I'll be back in an hour. Do you need anything?"

She wanted to say she needed him. *Just him.*

But one step at a time.

"Sure. I'd love some—"

"Rocky road ice cream?" he interrupted. "Snowman's

Creamery here makes some of the best ice cream you'll ever taste."

She gave him a thumbs-up and settled into the bed. Even though six months had passed since their relationship ended, this man still knew her so well. She should have never entertained the idea of marrying anybody else. There was no replacement for Nash Windham…well, Nash Fortune. None. And it was time for her to accept that. She didn't care what his name was. If she couldn't be with him, then she was better off alone.

Chapter Five

"I don't think I'll ever tire of becoming a grandmother," Wendy said, gushing, as she smoothed her black fitted pants and observed Colt in the bassinet.

Both baby and mom were now asleep in the aftermath of his family descending on the County General maternity ward to visit the newest Fortune. And reconnect with Imani. Nash had lost count of the pats on the back he had received, along with remarks like "you'd better keep her around this time."

He had snorted before reiterating that their breakup had been mutual. Not that anyone in his family listened or cared. They had been too enamored with his son. Right along with Nash. He kept looking at the perfect specimen he and Imani had produced.

A heady combination of awe, wonder and fear nearly brought him to his knees. His siblings had only been there for an hour but when they left, the room was filled with flowers, fruit, helium balloons and cute stuffed animals.

Colt yawned and rubbed his eyes before smiling.

Nash snapped a picture to add to the four hundred he probably had in his phone. "I'm fascinated and proud of everything he does," he whispered.

His mother touched his arm and said softly, "Spoken like a true father."

"Can't say the same about my own father." Bitterness weighed down his chest like a boulder on a feather.

"No one is all bad," Wendy reminded him, patting her shoulder-length bob. "I see my children as the best of both of us."

His lips quirked. "Mom, you're the queen of optimism."

"Well, sometimes life gives you a second chance and you have to learn to take it when it comes."

Nash cocked his head. Something about her tone made him feel like she wasn't just talking about him. "Anything you need to tell me? You've been real chipper lately."

Wendy played with her shirt collar but didn't meet his eyes. "I'm just happy for my children, that's all." Then she quickly changed topics. "I think it's great Imani is back in your life."

"Okay, Mom. But you know this is just temporary, right? She's staying with me at the guesthouse for a little bit. So this reunion is very much about Colt." A picture of him and Imani reminiscing earlier about their ice-cream dates as a couple hit his mind. He hadn't had that much fun on an actual date since they parted ways.

"If that's what you believe, I won't argue," Wendy said in a singsong voice, her green eyes sparkling. Imani stirred and his mom gestured toward the door. They crept outside the room, making sure to dim the lights. "You have to get the guesthouse ready."

His brow furrowed. "What do you mean? I just had it cleaned from top to bottom a couple weeks ago. It's move-in ready."

"That's not what I meant." She clucked her tongue. "Colt might be tiny but he comes with serious baggage." She counted her fingers as she rattled off a list. "You'll need a crib, a bassinet, car seat, diapers and wipes, bottles—"

"She's breastfeeding," he interjected, rubbing his eyes. What a lengthy list, and she sounded as if she could keep going. His heart thumped. What had he gotten himself into?

Wendy rolled her eyes. "If that baby is anything like you, she'll need to supplement with bottles. Or she'll be a zombie trying to feed him." She chuckled and tipped back her head. "You sure had a hearty appetite." She sighed, caught up in her memories. "I can still remember the day I brought you and Jade home. I held you both in my arms against my chest, with you wiggling against me. You looked at me like I was your favorite person in the whole world." Her eyes popped open, slightly misted. "Now, look at you. Over six feet tall."

Nash smiled despite himself. His mother had a way of making him feel like he could do anything. Like be a father to his son. "Mom, you're gushing over something I couldn't control. My height is based on genetics."

"Doesn't make me any less proud. You'll see the same thing with Colt. The smallest thing they do is remarkable." She pinned him with a gaze. "That feeling doesn't change as they grow older, either."

"I think I know what you mean." He grinned. "Colt burped after Imani fed him. *Burped*. And I kid you not, I felt pride hit my chest."

Wendy cracked up. "Yes! And when he wraps that tiny hand around your finger, your heart will twist, and you'll know for sure there's nothing you won't do for him."

Standing there with his mother, he felt confident. Wendy had a strong will and a quiet strength that he had drawn from when he was a child. And even now, she always knew what he needed to hear and the precise moment he needed to hear it. Leaning into her words, Nash believed he could do this father thing.

Perhaps not so much over the next couple of days, when he decided to tackle things off the extensive list Wendy had texted him before leaving the hospital. Plus, his son was getting circumcised this morning and that made his gut tighten.

Nash stood in the baby section at GreatStore by the strollers and car seats, and rubbed his temples. He had been there for an hour reading the different advantages of this brand and that brand, until everything became a blur. The salesperson had been patient, but he couldn't make up his mind. Having lots of choices wasn't always good. He had immediately sent out a distress signal.

Thankfully, his two younger sisters were on their way. Nash exhaled. With the fraternal twins, Dahlia and Sabrina, coming to take charge, all he would need to do is the heavy lifting and hand over his credit card, which was perfect.

His mother was already at his guesthouse to begin decorating, as she had ordered all sorts of things using next-day delivery. Wendy had texted him to choose a theme—stripes, safari, Southwestern—but in the end, Nash had told her to go with blue and white. All she had done was sent him a thumbs-up emoji. He prayed she kept it simple, all the while knowing she wouldn't. Wendy had already knitted the baby a huge blanket with the name *Colt* embroidered on it. How she had gotten that done in two days was beyond his comprehension.

But he was grateful.

"Hey! The helping brigade is here," Dahlia called out with a wave. Goodness, she was looking more and more like Mom all day. All of his sisters, except for Jade, had inherited their blond hair and tall, willowy figures from Wendy, although Dahlia normally wore her hair long in a low ponytail while Sabrina tended to keep shoulder-length curls. Dahlia had Wendy's presence, and her resilience, while Sabrina had his mother's sense of humor.

"How you doing, Dad, Daddy, Papa, Pop," Sabrina teased, her hazel eyes twinkling. She rested a hand on her rounded stomach. She was engaged, pregnant with twins, and Nash couldn't tell when he had seen his sister look more lovely… or happy.

"Have you decided what you want to be called yet?" Dahlia asked. She pointed to a car-seat-stroller combo and Nash obliged, placing it on the flatbed.

"No, I have no idea what Colt will call me. I don't know if I'll be around when he starts talking to make a decision. Maybe I'll suck at this and Imani will cut ties with me." He busied himself by reaching above Sabrina's head to get the bassinet. He wasn't about to let either of his sisters pick up any of the heavy items.

"Nonsense," Sabrina said. "You'll get the swing of things."

"Yeah, your worries are unfounded," Dahlia added.

"Unfounded?" he asked. "Did you forget about who our father was?"

"Did you forget about our mother?" Dahlia snapped back, her piercing blue eyes ablaze.

"Can we talk about more pleasant things?" Sabrina said. "Like how adorable Colt is and how Imani looks positively radiant for someone who just delivered." She rubbed her tummy.

"I have to agree. Colt is…perfect. And, Imani, well, she's never looked more beautiful to me," Nash said proudly, pulling up his phone to share pictures of Imani and Nash. As he continued piling the flatbed with baby gear, Sabrina snagged an empty cart and began filling it with baby wipes, diapers and bottles.

"Are you two getting back together?" Dahlia blurted.

His heart twisted. "No. We're just cohabitating and co-parenting for now." How hollow that sounded.

Sabrina raised an eyebrow. "Are you good with that?"

He wasn't too sure how he felt, but the past two days had been a whirlwind and he had to settle into the idea of parenting before he could tackle the question of his relationship status with Imani. "It's what's best for now," he said instead.

Luckily, his sisters didn't press further, and Nash left them gawking over the baby clothes—never mind that he had ordered a miniature Dallas Cowboys jersey online—and headed over to the grocery aisles. GreatStore was the primary place to buy anything and everything in Chatelaine. Nash waved at Paul, the general manager, before making his way through each aisle as they picked up all of Imani's favorites. Then he added a few ingredients to make her his special vegetable lasagna.

Imani wasn't a fan of vegetables. She only liked brussels sprouts (odd) and carrots mainly, but she would eat every single vegetable he put into his dish. He gathered the Parmesan, mozzarella, provolone and ricotta cheeses that he would need. He was almost certain he had pasta sauce and noodles at home. Nash planned to have it ready by the time she was discharged. Then maybe they could curl up by the fire and snuggle like old times once the baby was asleep.

A clank against his cart made him jump. It was his sisters. With the baby goods. This was about fulfilling his *son's* needs. Not his. He'd better keep that at the forefront of his mind. Because to get back with Imani meant giving her the whole shebang—love, marriage and, well, he'd already done the baby carriage.

But he couldn't be the father Colt needed. No matter what his mother or his sisters believed, he knew the truth.

Deep down, he believed that he lacked the ability to be a good father. He was positive that the worst thing he could do for Colt was remain in his son's life. So he would soak up these few months, and whenever Imani was ready, he would let them go. His gut twisted.

Easy to say but it was going to be hard to do.

But he would. Nash already loved Colt too much to ruin his future.

Chapter Six

"Awww. Why did they have to do my son like that?" Imani sniffled and looked at her mom for answers.

Abena and Zuri had driven to Chatelaine Hills to visit with her the night before, alternating between fussing at her for running off and hugging her with relief that she was safe. That Colt was here and doing well. Then they had stayed the night at the Chatelaine Hills Hotel and Resort, the only one in town.

Her grandmother had stayed behind at the resort this morning to work out. For an octogenarian, Zuri was extremely fit. Nothing interfered with her routine. She ran two to three miles and did close to fifty squats a day, keeping her legs and abs well-toned. She had passed on her love for running to all her grandchildren, though they weren't as disciplined. Zuri had even encouraged Abena to take up the sport.

Thinking of her mom and grandmother, Imani smiled. When she was younger, she believed Zuri was actually her mom's mother because they were that close. Abena confided that their bond was cemented because of loss on both their sides. Abena had lost her mother when she was a teen and Zuri had miscarried a daughter, making Phillip an only child.

Imani wrapped her son close to her bosom and kissed

his little head. His body shook from his tears. The obstetrician had returned with Colt, who was all red-faced from screaming after his circumcision, and her heart ached seeing him so distressed.

"You just have to nurse him and all will be well with his world," her mother said, seated across from her. She ran her fingers through her locs, which hung past her shoulders. "He won't remember it."

Imani had inherited Abena's high cheekbones, bronzed skin, narrow waist and wide hips. They were even the same size and height, both standing at five feet eight inches, which Imani loved once she was grown, because her mother's wardrobe was banging. Abena was always coordinated and well put together. They shared similar tastes, but her mom definitely veered toward the more refined, suitable for the daughter and wife of successful businessmen, while Imani's style could best be described as comfy chic.

She ran a hand through Colt's curls, watching his lower lip tremble. He hiccupped. "Hush, Mommy's baby. It's going to be okay." Soon, he latched on and his cries eased.

"Where's his father?" Abena asked, swinging a leg that showcased those ridiculous high heels she always wore. Her mom had on a two-piece royal blue pantsuit with a crisp white shirt and accessories that were an exact match with her color scheme.

"Nash was here early this morning, but he left to get his guesthouse ready for me and Colt, since we're getting discharged today." Which reminded her. Imani texted Nash a picture of Colt, now that he had calmed. Nash had low-key freaked out at the thought of his son getting circumcised, fleeing to go shopping for baby supplies and to set up the nursery. Not that that task didn't need to be done but he could have done it *later*.

Our little champion, Nash texted, along with a muscle-arm emoji.

Imani smiled. That he was.

Once Colt's breathing slowed and he fell into a slumber, Imani placed the baby in the bassinet and went to take a seat in one of the chairs by the window. Before she forgot, she also texted her father the same picture she had sent to Nash, although she was sure her mother had sent Phillip plenty of photos as well. The sun was out, and the skyline was filled with hues of blues that would make an amazing stock photo. Abena took out her hairbrush, oil and edge tamer and started working on Imani's curls.

"Thanks, Mama."

"Of course. You know I can't have you looking a hot mess. Do you want braids or a bun?" She gave Imani's hair a vigorous brush.

"A bun is fine. Wait… Braids." That way she wouldn't have to worry about fixing her hair for a few days and she could devote all her energy to taking care of Colt.

"Braids it is." Her mother got to work, parting her hair. "Have you spoken to Simon at all?"

"No, I blocked him after he texted me saying that we could still go through with the wedding." She bit her lip. "I really mucked things up."

Abena gave her shoulders a squeeze. "I'm sure that cat will land on his feet. Don't give him a second thought. I know you were friends since college but I never liked him. I always thought he had ulterior motives. It's going to be rocky for a while but I'm sure you'll find your way." Then she asked, "Is Nash going to take off from work to help you?"

"Yes, I think so. At least for the first few days. Then I don't know… We didn't finalize anything."

Abena tilted Imani's head and began the first braid, her hands moving fast. "I would have thought delivering his own baby would put things in perspective for him."

She didn't have to see her mother's face to know her lips were pursed. The classic sign of Abena's displeasure. Plus, that long, exaggerated sigh. "What do you expect? That he's going to ask me to marry him because I birthed his child? A child he told me didn't want? He has a real fear of messing up. His father did a number on him."

"I get it. But that will all change the more he's around his child." Her mom started on the second braid.

"And what if it doesn't? I can't be with someone who might resent me for making him take on a responsibility he didn't want."

"Nash might be a tad bit unsure, but he will come around. The man asked you to move into his guesthouse after all. His mouth might be saying he's scared, but his actions are showing he very much wants you around..."

"I know he wants me. I've never had any doubts about that." She touched her chest. "It's Colt I'm worried about. My desire to have children is literally the reason we broke up. But since he found out, Nash has been doing all the right things—he gave Colt the Fortune name, a place to live and he's out there buying supplies to get our son all he needs." Her voice hitched. "But will he give Colt his time—*quality* time? And will he give him his whole heart? Those are the questions I have."

Abena rubbed her back. "Ah, my child. I get it. I get it. Only time will answer those."

"I mean, I'm sure he has the best intentions, but that might not be enough." She dabbed at her eyes. "Are you and Grandma planning to stay with us? I'm sure I'm going to need your help."

"Yes, we will come to help. But we'll stay at the resort so you and Nash can settle in, spend time with your son as parents. I won't be far away if you need me." Abena brushed a few knots out of her hair before starting on the second-to-last braid.

Imani's cell phone buzzed. It was Nia video-calling from Paris. "Did you get the pictures I sent? Are you calling to see your new cousin?"

"I did and I can't wait to squeeze those cheeks," her cousin said with a frown. Abena gave Nia a wave before mouthing that she would be back.

"Is everything alright?" Imani asked once her mother had left the room.

"No. I just got a call from our warehouse assistant manager. Brad didn't show up to supervise the unloading." Brad was the manager and Imani had been counting on him to be there today.

"*Say what!* I can't believe he flaked like that," she whisper-yelled, slaking a glance Colt's way. His little body rose and fell and she sighed with relief. The last thing she wanted was to jolt her baby out of his sleep.

Nia ran a hand through her curls. "It's okay. I walked his assistant, Stella, through what needed to be done. I'll wrap things up here and come home on the next flight."

Her cousin sounded exhausted. "I can handle the meetings until you return," Imani offered.

"No, you're now officially out on maternity leave. Focus on the baby and I'll figure things out." Her brow furrowed. "Hang on. I didn't check my email until just now." She started tapping the screen.

Imani waited for her cousin to share the contents.

"Oh, snap! Our plans for expanding Lullababies to host

elite baby showers have been approved. We can begin construction as soon as we have secured all the permits."

"Wow." Her heart thumped.

Once again, Nia tapped away at the screen. "Don't worry yourself about this, cuz. I'll schedule discussions when I return."

Imani bit her lower lip. This baby boutique had been her dream for so long. She had used her trust fund when she came of age to chart her own path—and Nia had been the perfect business partner. Her cousin had a degree in fashion, specializing in merchandising and textiles. With Imani's business acumen and Nia's creativity, Lullababies had blossomed, and now, they would be taking on another venture. She felt a pang that she would be missing out on negotiations, but another glance Colt's way made her decision easy. "Go ahead. Don't put it off. Just keep me posted." Her voice cracked a little.

"Alright," Nia replied, and whooped. "I'll set up talks and send you updates along the way." Imani nodded, bunching her lips, her eyes misting. Nia must have misinterpreted her reaction because she said, "Imani, I've got this. You can trust me. I know this store is your heart, your baby. I won't fail you, I promise."

Imani drew in a deep breath. "I trust you. It's not that. It's…" Her stomach knotted. She couldn't say the words she knew she wanted to say just yet. "I know Lullababies is in good hands. I'll look out for your updates." Then she ended the call.

She walked over to the bassinet to check on her baby. Needing the physical contact, she rubbed Colt's head. That very act centered her.

"What's going on?" Abena asked, coming back inside with a fruit cup for Imani and a yogurt for herself.

Imani wrapped her arms about herself. "Lullababies is about to blow up." She filled her mother in on the expansion plans, then added, "Actually, speaking of Nia, I'm thinking of leaving her in charge and selling her my shares, once the expansion is finished."

Abena's eyes widened. "Are you sure you want to do that? You guys worked your butts off and I'm proud of you." She flailed her hands. "I'll support you either way but give it serious thought. Besides, your hormones need to settle before you make that kind of a decision." Her mother could be right. Abena often was. But when Nia called the store "her baby," Imani knew that was no longer true. Colt now filled that space.

Abena beckoned her back to the chair. "Come. Let me finish your braids. When the time comes, you'll know what to do." Imani gave a jerky nod and returned to her position. Her mother gave her a hug before finishing up her hair. Abena must have known she needed to process, because she hummed some random tune but didn't continue making conversation.

Until recently, Imani had worked sixteen- to eighteen-hour days easily. But she hadn't thought about her store at all during the past few days. Granted, she had just given birth, but once she'd held Colt in her arms, her priorities had shifted.

She knew she wanted to be there for all of Colt's firsts.

And…didn't Nash deserve the same opportunity?

Wait… What was she saying? She mentally backtracked, rubbing her eyes. Imani was getting ahead of herself. She didn't know if Nash would truly embrace fatherhood once the thrill of Colt's arrival waned.

Imani released a plume of air. She anticipated every single moment of raising their son—the highs, the lows and everything in between—and could only hope Nash would as well. But that was up to him. They would be at his guest-house long enough for those questions to be answered. And all she could do was wait.

Wait, and pray that Nash accepted his rightful place in his son's life.

Chapter Seven

With the fridge stocked and the nursery complete, all Nash had left to do was move his family into his home. Yet he was petrified. He'd never shared his private space full-time with anyone. Since moving out of his mother's home, Imani had been the closest he had come to living with a woman.

Imani, he could do.

Imani and Colt, however, were an entirely different dynamic.

Still, Nash engaged in a steady stream of conversation with his baby mama as he drove them home from the hospital later that evening. He had already shared about his father's death and the family's decision to purchase the ranch. He didn't know how she didn't hear his heart galloping inside his chest as each mile brought him closer to the Fortune family compound.

"So tell me about your family ranch," Imani said, wiping at a speck of lint on her jeans. She had on a pretty, long-sleeved blouse with sunflower-shaped buttons.

"Well, it's about thirty-five hundred acres and if you ask me, it was like it was made for us."

She gasped. "Thirty-five hundred acres? Wow. I can't even picture how big it must be. You guys must have to drive everywhere."

"It's huge. We mostly used golf carts to get around the

ranch. There's a main house, and then there are six log cabins that each of us occupy."

He drove through the iron gates and the huge awning at the entrance that boasted their new ranch sign. Imani straightened and looked outside the window, her mouth agape. It was dusk, so the oranges and purples of the vibrant autumn Texas landscape made for a majestic sight as he made his way down the half-mile strip leading to the ranch itself. He took in the fields on each of their sides, his chest puffing at its resplendence.

When he came to the fork in the road, Nash decided to go left to give her a driving tour, pointing out the stables, the barns, the cattle and horses grazing.

"How many people do you employ for upkeep?"

"We have about fifteen new employees and a plethora of day hires—people just passing through who want temporary work." He stopped to show Imani the main house, which had been constructed using weathered light-colored stone, a sloped metal roof and wood finishes. The covered porch extended from either side of the front door and had six posts and a white railing.

"There's a dirt back road directly from the ranch to my house, but I drive this way home sometimes."

"Yeah, so now that I'm not swimming through an abundance of hormones, why don't you bring me up to speed on this name change and how you all ended up here."

Nash pulled away from where he'd parked. "My mom's the best person to tell this story because it's quite fascinating, but I'll do my best." He cleared his throat. "Wendell Fortune—that's the grandfather my mother was named after—had a secret illegitimate daughter, Ariella McQueen. Ariella was in love with a poor miner, which Wendell didn't approve of, and she ended up getting pregnant—a pregnancy she hid from everyone. With her mother deceased, Ariella really wanted to please Wendell and have him acknowledge her existence, which he refused."

Imani's eyes went wide. "Goodness. This is like a storyline from my mother's soaps. Too bad I don't have any ice cream."

Nash chuckled. "When the baby was a month old, Ariella decided to choose love over a relationship with Wendell and went to the mine to get her lover, so that they could elope. She left her baby girl with a sitter named Gertie Wilson. Gertie was the only person who knew of the baby's existence. But Ariella did write a letter to Wendell telling him of her plans and confessing that she had given birth to a daughter—his grandchild. But Wendell never actually read that letter. He kept it but said he was afraid to open it and read what was inside."

"Wow. I wonder how Ariella hid the pregnancy?" Imani asked, before waving him on to continue.

"Unfortunately, we will never know because Ariella was one of fifty-one people who lost their lives in a mining disaster that very same day."

"Oh, my." Imani wrapped her arms about her. "I'm sorry to hear that. Ariella was your grandmother, correct?"

"Yes, but it's okay. I didn't know her."

"Wait, rewind. So what happened to the baby back then?" Imani rubbed her chin. "I mean, I realized the baby is Wendy, but I guess my real question is, how did Wendy find out she's Wendell's granddaughter?"

"Good question." He squared his shoulders, his fingers drumming on the steering wheel. "Right…so when Ariella didn't return, Gertie believed the baby was abandoned. Since no one knew of the baby's existence, Gertie moved hours away and raised my mother as her own, as Wendy

Wilson. It wasn't until she died six months ago that my mother learned the truth. Gertie had left her a letter confessing everything."

Imani released a long breath. "Whew. Wow. That's something. Two letters bearing some tough truths."

"Yes, which is why I hate secrets." He shook his head. "No one thinks of the damage they bring to the next generation. Imagine learning that your grandma isn't really your grandma."

She gave his hand a squeeze. "I wish I had been there for you."

"Me, too." He exhaled. "But, when my mother contacted Wendell with her discovery, he confirmed its veracity by sharing the letter from Ariella." He dabbed at his eyes. "That was one massive family reunion, let me tell you."

"I'm so glad this story led to a happy ending for you, your siblings and your mom."

"Yes, and in addition to gaining family, my mother inherited Fortune's Castle in Chatelaine."

Imani's mouth dropped. "You guys have a real-life castle? That's some whole other level of wealth right there."

"I guess." He could feel his face heat.

"My mother had the number fifty-one etched into the cement to honor my grandmother and the others who died in the mining disaster and is currently in the process of transforming the castle into a luxury hotel, suite of offices and venue for events. Then she purchased this place for all of us and we took on the Fortune name, which you already know about."

"Yes, and this ranch is *enormous*. What a place to come home to," she breathed out, then he mentioned that the lake separated Chatelaine Hills from the town of Chatelaine.

His heart filled. "I love that me and my siblings all live

together, but with enough space between us so we're not in each other's way." Nash returned to the entrance and this time took a right turn by the lake.

He passed Jade's home first, then turned toward his own entrance. He drove through the metal gate and the stone pillars. His house was recessed farther than the others, hidden from the main path. There was also a wall of privacy trees surrounding the property.

Imani's breath caught. "This is what you call a *cabin*? It's more like a waterfront mansion with log exteriors." She placed a hand to her chest. "When you said you lived on a ranch, I didn't envision anything this fancy."

"I guess. I have four bedrooms in mine, but some of the others have six." He pulled next to his golf cart and parked, intending to give her a tour of his home. He couldn't wait to show her the 1980 Jaguar that he had had restored. When they dated, Nash had told Imani how much he wanted to own one. They had brainstormed everything from the dark green color and gold trimming as a must-have, to the places where they would go in it. The sports car now sat in his garage, though he had only driven it once. Maybe he had been waiting for Imani and he didn't realize it. Excitement flowed as he envisioned seeing her face when she sat on the plush leather seat for the very first time.

Just then, Colt started fussing in the back seat. He swallowed his disappointment and gave her an apologetic smile. "Rain check? We can tour my home another time. I imagine you want to get settled in and Little Man needs your attention." She raised an eyebrow and he slapped his forehead. "I meant *our* attention." He peeked behind him and saw Colt still had his eyes closed. "He's not fully awake yet," Nash whispered.

The baby whined.

"Yes, he's probably hungry and needs a diaper change." He could hear the worry in her tone.

Nash felt a surge of protectiveness and patted her leg. "He's okay." He hoped. What did he know?

"Yes, you're right," she said, obviously trying to sound brave. "Crying is how they communicate. You can change Colt and I will search for something to munch on while I'm nursing."

"That will work," he squeaked out, wiping his palm on his leg. Nash started up the Range Rover and backed out— the only sound now was the gravel of the packed earth beneath his tires. Then he drove around to the guesthouse, this time, taking the only other spot next to her Jeep.

They heard a small whimper.

"Perfect timing," she said, opening her door—before he could do it for her.

Nash lifted a hand and went to lift the car seat. Taking Imani's hand, he led her up the small path and opened the door. Colt was now crying at a louder volume. Nash gripped the car seat and took him inside.

Colt bunched his fists and stiffened before he wailed.

A full-fledged red-in-the-face wail. Dang, this child went from calm to storm in under sixty seconds. Nash rested him on the couch and stepped back.

"Somebody's impatient," Imani cooed, reaching down to unbuckle her son. Then she held up the bundle in Nash's direction.

His heart thundered and he gave Imani a look. "I don't know what to do."

"Can you change his diaper?" she asked. "I've got to use the bathroom."

"Sure. The bathroom's down the hallway on your right." He held the baby close and Colt calmed a little, his little mouth searching. "Um, I don't have what you're looking for." It was like Colt understood him because he started to cry. Nash realized that he hadn't grabbed any of the baby's things from his car, including the diaper bag. What should he do?

Maybe he was holding him wrong. He placed the crying bundle back into the car seat and clenched his jaw. Imani sure was taking a long time in the bathroom. Did she leave him alone with Colt on purpose? His brow furrowed. *"Imani!"* he yelled, panic pumping through his veins.

"I'm coming," she yelled back. He could hear the toilet flush and the water running.

"I'm out of my league here." Nash wiped his brow. Colt had now squirmed so much that he had ended up in an awkward position. "I left the diaper bag in the car."

Imani rushed over and gathered the newborn in her arms. She sounded out of breath and cross with him. "I'm sure there are diapers in the nursery. Why didn't you just rock him or something, then? I was gone less than a minute."

Though she asked that question, what Nash heard was, *Why do you suck at this already?*

He jutted his jaw and stormed outside to get the baby's possessions, furious at her and himself. His chest heaved. He told Imani months ago that fatherhood wasn't for him and what did she do? Sprang a baby on him and expected him to be a contender for father of the year. He didn't know a daggone thing about babies. Nash placed both hands on the rear of the Range Rover and drew deep breaths. He hated the surly thoughts flowing through his mind and needed to redirect before he said something he regretted.

Inhale. Imani hadn't gotten pregnant by herself.

Exhale. Colt didn't ask to be here.

Inhale. Imani was here because he had invited her.

Exhale. Colt was a baby and, what did Imani say? He was crying to communicate.

His panic ebbed. Knowing he couldn't stall any longer, Nash opened the trunk and filled his arms with as much stuff as he could take in one trip and headed back into the house. Colt was contentedly nursing while Imani sang to him. "He couldn't wait to eat. I'll change him after."

Envy slapped him in the gut. Imani was born for motherhood. While he was just woefully inadequate. Nash placed the baby bag next to her, unable to look her in the eyes.

His cell phone pinged. There was a text from Ridge. His brother was on his way to his house. *Lifesaver.* "I've got to head out but I'll be back to check up on you." Or maybe he would just call instead. Yeah. That was a much better plan.

"Alright," Imani said, giving him a beatific smile. "We'll be here."

Nash went to the fridge to get her cheese sticks, apple slices and yogurt. The delight on her face proved he could do right when it came to Imani. His son, not so much.

Helplessness and guilt made his steps heavy as he walked to his house, taking the stairs to his multilevel deck and entering through the sliding door and into the kitchen. Placing his hands on the granite countertop, Nash pictured the seven-pounder in his guesthouse who made him quake and fumble. If his mother had been here, he would be bending her ear right now.

He heard a rap on the door and shook his head, his curls cascading in his face. "Come in," he hollered, knowing it was Ridge. Nash ran a hand through his unruly hair. He needed a trim.

"Hey, bro, how's fatherhood treating you?" Tall and lanky, Ridge was the youngest of the six siblings. He held a small package in his hand—which Nash assumed was another gift for Colt.

"I'm a wreck right now," he confessed, dipping his head to his chest. "It hasn't even been five minutes and I'm already screwing up. Just like Dad." Nash then told his younger brother what had transpired moments before in the guesthouse.

"Aww. You'll get the hang of it, bro, but you've got to leave Dad out of this."

Nash's head popped up. Ridge spoke with certainty, his brown eyes earnest. The certainty of *current* experience. The past few months, Ridge had been helping to take care of baby Evie while Hope waited for the return of her memories.

After placing the package on the countertop, his brother strutted over to give his shoulder a squeeze.

Ridge thumped his chest. "Evie isn't even my child and I feel so much for her—a natural protectiveness, a surge of love. Fatherhood is a combination of instinct and hands-on learning. I've had a huge learning curve, but I made a conscious choice to be the kind of father figure Evie needs right now during this strange time that Hope is in my life," his said, his voice full of steel, "for as long as she needs me. And Casper Windham doesn't dictate what I do from the grave."

To hear the family heartbreaker, who ran from any form of commitment, speak with such conviction really moved Nash. His brother had matured in character since acquiring a ready-made family and Nash felt nothing but pride about that.

"That's great, bro. I just wish it were that simple for me…that I could will myself to be a good father to Colt. To be honest, I'm all discombobulated over this. Nothing I'm experiencing so far with fatherhood feels instinctual." He jabbed a finger to his chest. "Yes, I felt a bond the moment I held Colt in my arms. But all I feel about parenthood in the long years to come is fear and dread."

"I, too, am experiencing moments of fear and dread," Ridge admitted. "But it's at the thought of losing Hope and Evie when her memory fully returns." He chuckled. "I've kinda gotten used to having them around."

Whoa. It was evident that Ridge had strong feelings for Hope and Evie. Nash's heart squeezed. "Have there been any new developments with her regaining her memory?" he asked gently.

Ridge shifted and rubbed his chin. "She has flashes of memory and it's clear she's running from something," he said, his voice filled with unease, "but what she's running from, I have no idea."

That had to be tough. "Yet you're still putting yourself out there with Evie…?"

"Yeah, and though I have no idea what lies ahead, I'd do it again."

Nash drummed the countertop with his fingers. "That's remarkable." He pinned his brother with a gaze. "*You're* remarkable."

Ridge shrugged, his skin reddening. "Yeah, well, this might be the dumbest and bravest thing I've ever done in my life. But at least I'll have no regrets."

"Good for you." Nash hugged him close. "Just know that the entire family, especially me, is rooting for you. You have my support."

"I appreciate that." Ending the embrace, Ridge cocked his head. "You have my support as well. Love on that baby," he said, his voice cracking a little, "especially since you know for sure he's yours."

In other words, unlike Ridge, Nash didn't have to worry about another daddy popping up and taking his family from him. "Hang in there," he told him. His brother left after that and Nash mulled over Ridge's passionately spoken words about having no regrets. Nash needed to be able to say the same when it came to Colt.

He bunched his fists—ready or not, he had to at least try. For Colt's sake as well as his own. But he wasn't about to show up empty-handed.

Chapter Eight

Her baby could die if she closed her eyes. If only the nurse hadn't mentioned SIDS when she was in the hospital, then maybe Imani wouldn't have done some research and now she wouldn't be all paranoid that her child could become a horrible statistic. Especially since it was more common in boys than girls.

Ugh, she should have avoided the internet search. Why didn't anybody tell her not to do that? Not that she would have listened.

Fear cloaked her heart, and she couldn't shake it off no matter how much she tried. Now, her heart clamored in her chest and her eyelids burned. Because she couldn't get to sleep!

Imani had placed Colt next to her on the king-size bed so she could watch him breathe. He was holding his breath for about two seconds and then expelling the air out of his body in one whoosh. Was that normal? She didn't know and she didn't want to look it up because that's how she'd ended up here.

It was close to 11:00 p.m. and she had been up since 5:00 a.m. that morning and Nash hadn't returned yet, like he'd promised. *Yet?* She was kidding herself to think he would. Nash had dashed out of the guesthouse within minutes of their arrival, leaving her alone to figure things out with their newborn. Imani hadn't dared call her mother because, well, she didn't want Abena thinking badly of Nash. She sniffled and wiped her face.

Colt released shallow, staccato breaths.

Oh, goodness, her body shuddered. He wasn't breathing properly. Something might be wrong with his lungs.

Maybe she could call the pediatrician to find out.

Her cell phone chimed with a text from Nash. You up?

Yes. Are you com— She deleted. Don't want to pressure him.

With a sigh, she just texted, Yes.

Okay. I'm on my way.

It's about time, she typed. *Delete. Delete. Delete.* Instead, she texted, Let yourself in, then placed the baby in the bassinet, which she had moved into her bedroom. Then, after grabbing the baby monitor, she went into the living area to wait for him. Nash had installed cameras around the circumference of the property and in the nursery, but Colt was too young to be in that big old space by himself, no matter how lovely it was.

She heard a whimper and skedaddled back into the bedroom, slightly out of breath.

To her relief, she saw Colt's little chest was rising and falling with those little fists in the air. Aww. *My sweet baby.* Imani took what had to be picture number five hundred and eighty-seven and settled back on the bed to continue her vigil. As soon as Nash entered the room, holding a huge bouquet of flowers, she released a long exhale.

"I'm so glad you're here," she choked out, suddenly overcome at being able to voice her fears aloud. "I'm so scared."

Nash rested the floral arrangement on the nightstand,

then came to sit on the bed and took her hand. "What's wrong?"

"C-Colt c-could die a-any minute." She flung herself into Nash's arms. His hands rubbed her back and she breathed in his masculine scent. Being in his arms soothed her. "K-keep an eye on h-him," she hiccupped. "I j-just need a minute." Then she sobbed, the fears oozing out of her shaking body as his arms grounded her.

She felt a kiss on the top of her head. "What's going on?"

Imani pulled out of his embrace, squared her shoulders and shared what she had found out about SIDS. His eyes went wide and his brow furrowed. But then he shook his head. "My mother had six children and we all turned out fine. I know it's a reality, but I choose to believe that Colt will thrive. You did. I did." He pointed at Colt. "And, he will, too."

She rubbed her eyes, dried out from all that crying. "You sound really sure. But there are no guarantees."

"Do you want me to call my mom?" Nash asked, looking at his watch. "Or get you some ice cream?"

"No. No. She might be asleep. That's why I didn't bother my family. And if I eat ice cream feeling this way, my tummy might get upset. I—I'd rather stay up until daybreak, or we take turns watching him."

"Alright, if that's what you want, then that's what we'll do," Nash said. "If it's okay with you, I'll stay here and I'll take the first shift. You get some sleep."

Grateful, Imani gave a jerky nod and snuggled in his arms. "Wake me up if he needs to feed."

He lifted a hand. "I can feed him. I saw the bottles you put in the fridge with the date and time labeled on them."

Imani had pumped for the first time that morning at the hospital, and while that task had been no easy feat, she wanted Nash to be able to feed Colt if he desired. When she had opened the fridge earlier to store the bottles, that's when she saw that Nash had purchased a lot of her favorites. She had gotten all mushy inside that he remembered what she liked. "Are you sure you're okay with feeding him tonight?" When he nodded, she asked, "You know how to use the bottle warmer?" Another nod. "You won't fall asleep?"

"No. I will be up. Get some rest. I won't let anything happen to our son."

Our son. Her heart warmed at him taking ownership. "You're going to be a great father."

"If you say so. The jury is still out on that one," he scoffed.

"Just give it a chance. By the way, that nursery is beyond my expectations. You didn't spare any expense." She yawned.

He preened. "Yeah, it turned out pretty good. Colt is worth every penny."

"Yes, but I'll speak for him until he can speak for himself. Colt would much prefer your time, your heart, over your money any day. All this—" she splayed her hands toward the baby paraphernalia in the bedroom "—is just… stuff." Her lips quirked. "Great stuff. Expensive stuff. But stuff, nonetheless. Material goods will never replace the security of having a father's unconditional love."

"I get that." She could tell from his tone that he was thinking of his own strained relationship with his father. Her heart squeezed. She couldn't bear her son growing up feeling the same about Nash the way that Nash felt about Casper Windham.

"You're a good man, Nash Fortune, or I wouldn't have come this close—" she brought her index finger and thumb close to each other "—to falling in love with you. I'm sure that goodness will transfer over to our baby boy."

Nash patted Cole's bum. "Okay, I'll do my best. I want to be there to meet all of his needs."

"I hope you feel that way when you have to get up in the middle of the night." Her eyelids fluttered closed.

Everything was going well. Until…it wasn't.

Imani lay snoring, her arm slung across her face. Nash quirked his lips. He had spent just as much time watching her as he had watching Colt. And he couldn't decide who was the cuter of the two.

It was the wee hours of the morning and Colt had awakened. Nash had been sitting up against the headboard on the other end of the bed, alternating between scrolling through his cell phone, reviewing his strategic plans with Arlo's comments and watching random baby videos—including one on learning CPR, because you never knew—when Colt stirred awake. Nash had looked over to see a pair of hazel eyes staring back at him. At least they looked hazel—he couldn't be sure.

That's when he sprang into action, going through his mental checklist so he got everything perfect.

He used the bottle warmer to warm the milk. Check. Not too cold. Not too hot. Just right.

He fed Colt. Check. Tummy nice and full.

He burped the baby. Check. Nice, strong burp.

Then after several YouTube video tutorials, Nash changed his son's diaper, even managed to get the diaper snug across his bottom, with no accidental whizzing. At this point, a solid hour had passed. Yet, here it was 5:28 a.m. and he couldn't get Colt to go back to sleep.

Sitting on one of the two rocking chairs in the nursery, Nash experienced none of the calm vibe the decor in the room was meant to solicit. Wendy had embraced a nautical theme—right in line with his choice of blue and white. Everything from the area rug, the lamps, the bedding, the matching accessories and the artwork, which he had hung, made Colt's room classy and organized. There was even a nook that held baby's first books and teddy bears, along with a sound system with the option of water waves or white noise—neither of which were working at the moment in settling his newborn.

Nash rocked. And patted. And rocked some more. Yet Colt was very much awake. And now, that cute face appeared scrunched and his stomach felt tight to the touch. Nash had a fussy baby on his hands.

With no clue what to do.

In an instant, Colt was screeching at the top of his lungs, and he had the wriggling tyke on his chest, his shirt getting wetter and wetter with tears. Nash decided to walk him, pacing back and forth before venturing into the living area.

"What's going on?" Imani said groggily.

He whipped around to see her standing there in just her black boy shorts and she had traded the blouse for a cotton maternity top. Dang, she looked good. Her hair was all messy and sexy, like she'd just rolled out of his bed. *Whoosh.* Nash licked his lips. He wanted to—

Colt must have heard Imani's voice because he stiffened and cried even louder.

"Let me hold him," Imani said, coming to his side. She took the baby from Nash, then cooed and snuggled Colt in her arms. "Is he hungry?"

"No. And I just changed him a few minutes ago." Nash's shoulders sagged. "I told you I'm no good at this." If he closed his eyes, he would fall right asleep.

"You're fine. He's just fussing, that's all." It took her a few minutes but Colt settled and went to sleep.

"No, I just don't have what it takes. This just proved it." Feelings of inadequacy overshadowed his earlier ones of competence. Or at least of surviving.

"Not from my perspective." Imani placed a finger over those enticing lips of hers and gestured for him to wait. Then she tiptoed into the bedroom to put Colt into the bassinet, and came back into the room a few minutes later with the baby monitor in hand.

Her face shone and she did a light jig, almost skipping over to him. His eyebrows knitted. Why was she so chipper? He hoped she wasn't about to brag on her parenting skills. "Guess what?" she asked, resting the baby monitor on the nightstand.

"Yeah. I know he's sleeping. I was right here when Colt's head lolled back and I could see the drool running down the side of his face." He glanced at the small screen. Gosh, Colt looked so cute.

"No, silly." Imani did some silent claps before gyrating her hips, then waving her hands in the air, going in beat to the water waves. Alright, she had his attention now.

Nash stood and stretched before joining her, spooning her from behind. He closed his eyes and allowed the beat of the water and the sounds of the waves to fill his senses. Their bodies took on a familiar rhythm, moving in sync, stirring emotions and heightening senses that had been in stasis. For six long months. He ground his hips against that firm butt and groaned.

Her arms circled his neck as his hands traveled the path from her abdomen under her shirt to give her full breasts a gentle squeeze, their larger size a perk of pregnancy.

He whispered in her ear. "Not that I mind, but what exactly are we celebrating?" His voice deepened with desire, electrical sparks igniting wherever they made contact.

"We survived Colt's first night home alone as parents and, most importantly, so did he. Colt's alive and breathing and my heart is doing somersaults right now." She spun to face him. "Three down and one hundred and fifty-seven to go."

"I don't get it."

"The risk of SIDS is higher between one and four months. We're on a countdown." She spun to face him. "And day three is in the bag, all thanks to you. You got me through the scariest night of my life."

Her breath was minty—but how? She must have brushed her teeth when she put Colt down to bed. He had brushed his with a spare toothbrush that he'd left for guests, and then helped himself to a small glass of orange juice, while he waited for Colt's bottle to warm.

He used an index finger to dip her chin toward him. "You can't do that, Imani. You can't count days, afraid of mortality. That's not living. You want to allow yourself to thrive in all the wonderful aspects of motherhood. I understand your anxiety. I feel it, too, but it can't consume you. It can't overshadow the good moments."

"You're right. I'll try." Imani relaxed her shoulders and molded her body into his, then tilted her head to look into his eyes. "You should do the same."

Pleasure infused his heart and his lower region. Nash's hands cupped her bottom, loving how they fit well into his palms. Aching need thrummed through every area of his body where they connected. If this had been many months back, he would be ridding them of their clothes to sink deeply into her soft, welcoming folds. But Imani had just given birth. His eyes dropped to her mouth. Judging by the invitation in her eyes, Imani was as caught up as he was and in agreement.

He caressed her face before gripping the back of her head. His hands caressed her soft curls, loving the scent of jasmine. Her lips parted.

What kind of man would he be if he didn't oblige?

Nash pressed his mouth to hers, desperate for another taste after so, so long. And, oh, she tasted so good. He feasted on those decadent, luscious lips. Passion ignited within him, his body remembering her achy sweetness, yearning for more.

He moved to end the kiss but she grabbed on, her tongue dueling with his, an unspoken challenge that he was determined to win. But then, she reached up to massage his earlobes. Goodness, she remembered his Achilles' heel. His toes curled in his boots and he stifled his moan. Nash knew he had to put an end to this sensual madness before he lost complete control.

After tearing his lips from hers, they faced off, chest heaving, panting, gasping for breath.

"Whoa, that was… I don't even have the words," he said, his mind scattered with his swirling thoughts.

She smirked. "That was long overdue." She passed by him and swatted him on the butt. "Now, go get you some sleep."

Nash yawned. "I probably should head down to the ranch. Arlo said he would cover for me, but I think I should at least show my face." He had been so caught up in Imani and Colt that he hadn't even checked on Stanley since the other man left the hospital. Plus, he had another new hire, Roger Pitts, that he needed to check on.

"You're the boss. You are entitled to take some kind of family leave," Imani said. "Plus, you'll be of no use to anyone if you're too exhausted."

By this time, sleep fanned at his eyes. "Alright. I'll be

back in a few. I'll get a nap and I'll be back over early afternoon. What do you want for lunch?"

"Sounds like a plan. And hmm…well, I've been craving a nice, juicy burger and a big plate of fries." She licked her lips.

"I'll pick some up on my way back."

"Awesome." She blew him a kiss and headed back into the room. "I'll put Colt's laundry on to wash and then I'm going right back to bed myself. The rule is, I should sleep when the baby sleeps and I'm going to try to follow that."

With a wave, Nash departed, walking out into the early sunrise, enjoying the autumn breeze and the breathtaking beauty of the fall season. The oak, cypress and maple trees produced vibrant hues of orange, yellow and red, a majestic view of transition. He stopped a moment to take in the chirr of the American robins and the peacefulness of the lake. Like his siblings, he had his boat tethered to the docking station. By now, Nash could barely keep his eyes open.

Instead of entering through the back, Nash walked around to the front of his home to get the morning paper. There was a young teen who delivered *The Chatelaine Daily News* before going to school. Nash hadn't heard the signature hum of the teen's doctored Mustang that morning. After bending over to pick up the paper, he used his phone to unlock the front door.

As soon as he closed the door behind him, Nash texted his brother for an update. Arlo replied immediately.

I've got it handled. Stanley called about coming back to work today. Dahlia convinced him to take leave. Everything is as it should be.

Alright. Reach out if you need me.

Will do… Do you need me to move the family meeting to the 15th?

Okay. That's not a bad idea.

I'm on it. Enjoy your family.

Family. Wow. In a matter of days, Nash had been given a family of his own. He stewed on that realization as he made his way up the stairs. Thanksgiving was a few weeks away and it would be nice to have Imani and Colt with him.

Nash sauntered down the hallway to his bedroom, done in beige and deep browns, with a couple of his ranch hats on the walls. But now, where there used to be a blank space, there was a picture of Colt. Beside it was a small picture of the baby's tiny feet on the left, and another smaller picture of Colt on the right. Funny. He didn't recall taking that picture. He moved close to investigate, then gasped.

That was him as a baby.

Colt was what Wendy would call his spitting image, the only difference being his son's olive-toned skin.

He staggered backward, until he touched the edge of the bed. Nash sank down on the mattress, gripping the comforter, and sat there in awe for a beat.

Imani's words came back to him. *Colt would much prefer your time, your heart, over your money any day.*

How many times had he felt those sentiments regarding his own father? Nash didn't want Colt to feel that pain of rejection, of not being good enough. He curled his lips inward, vowing to be there for his son. To be the role model Colt would need so that years from now, he wouldn't be in a similar position, questioning his ability to father his child.

Yes. He would do everything in his power to be the father for Colt that he wished Casper had been.

Nash eyed his son's picture as determination strengthened his will. Then he uttered, "I promise to do my best, son. I won't let you down. You're going to know you're loved by me, every single day." And he would start today.

Taking a chance, he called Imani's cell phone. "Everything okay?" she whispered. "Colt is still asleep."

"Yes, can you take a video call?"

"Sure, the laundry cycle just started. I thought you'd be knocked out by now."

A few seconds later, he was staring into Imani's sweet face, her eyes inquisitive. "Would you mind taking me to see Colt for a second?"

"He's still asleep."

"I know. I won't wake him." She did as he asked. As soon as Nash saw the infant, his heart expanded. In a hoarse whisper, Nash said, "I love you, son. Daddy loves you." When Imani turned the camera back to her, she had tears in her eyes. All she could do was nod, and he figured she was too emotional for words, which was alright, because so was he.

Chapter Nine

Why on earth couldn't Hammond Porter keep things simple?

Her grandfather had called to say that he was coming to visit and Imani had prepared lunch for two. Okay, so it was a bagged salad and premade grilled chicken strips, but in her defense, she was a new mom nursing a baby who needed to be fed every two hours. She honestly didn't think she had enough milk to sustain Colt's appetite and that made her heart ache. Made her feel like less than. But she planted a smile on her face and pushed all that aside since her grandfather was coming to visit.

She was looking forward to their lunch date, but hadn't expected to see three black Escalades pull in front of the guesthouse carrying her mother and grandmother, her two aunties, Mazie and Yemana, and five of her six cousins— Zaire, the twins, Kamara and Ashanti, Xavion and Omari. So much for an intimate family gathering. However, since each person carried a platter of some heavenly comfort food, she had forgiven him.

Besides, she hadn't had to change or feed her son once he had awakened from his nap. Her family, who assured her they were well and up-to-date on shots, had taken care of all of Colt's needs, giving her a much-needed respite.

Though she still had her qualms about so many people being around her newborn, at least they were family. Nash had helped himself to a plate then dashed off to the ranch, using the excuse of giving her private time with her peeps. And, yes, he had used the word *peeps*.

Exclaiming about the picturesque foliage lining the bank of the lake, Imani's cousins decided to venture out to explore the hiking trails on the ranch. Her mother and grandmother caught up on the latest episode of their favorite soap opera, and Auntie Mazie napped on the recliner. It was Auntie Yemana's turn to tend to Colt.

Since everyone was occupied, Grandpa beckoned to her to join him for a walk. They took the path down to the dock. He clasped his hands behind him. He was a stately man and looked more like sixty than the eighty-eight years he was. Hammond bench-pressed two-ninety and could still drop and give you twenty push-ups on command. What could she say—her grandparents personified her fitness goals.

Grandpa cleared his throat and stroked his pepper-gray beard. "I got a chance to talk with the board about my retirement next year and your taking the helm to continue my legacy."

"Oh?" Her eyebrows raised. "I don't imagine that went over well." The group of six men and one woman could best be described as archaic and stuffy.

Hammond cleared his throat. "Well, their exact words were 'Imani isn't qualified enough to take the reins of such an illustrious company.'"

"I can't say I disagree with them." They stopped by the lake to admire the calm waters. A couple wood ducks hovered close with about five ducklings behind them.

She shoved her hand in the pockets of her black-and-cream striped button-down dress, which she wore with slip-on shoes. Thank goodness, she still had the weekender, and shopping bags in her trunk. Plus, her mother had also brought a suitcase with more clothes for her extended stay. Imani touched her belly, feeling her luxury tummy shaper designed to feed her love for sexy underwear and get back her pre-pregnancy bod. It wouldn't take long, since she had run every morning up until seven months.

"Don't listen to those old fuddy-duddies. They are not going to tell me what to do with my company and I do think some of their concerns are plain old gender bias."

Imani turned to rest a hand on her grandpa's palm. "Even if they feel their opinion is based on my being a woman, you do need to see if their objections are valid." She squared her shoulders. "I don't think I'm the person for the job."

"Nonsense." Hammond gave a dismissive wave. "You are more than qualified. But I'm retiring, not dead. I'll be on hand to guide if you need. Though I doubt you will."

The one stubborn, and at times useful, quality about her grandfather was that he didn't quit. A necessary trait if you were going to maintain billionaire status. When he wanted something, he had tunnel vision. And she had no doubt Hammond was going to use his gift of gab to sweet-talk her into seeing things his way.

Before Colt, she would have caved.

But her priorities had shifted and she told her grandfather as much. "I don't want my business life to consume my personal one. I want to be present in my son's life to see every single milestone. Porters eat, sleep and play oil, and that's not me."

Hammond nodded with understanding but he wasn't easily thwarted. "How about we do this instead? Let me scout around for a suitable replacement over the next few months. Once I'm gone that person can oversee the everyday operations, but then you would have the final vote. How does that sound?"

"What about Jonathan? He would be perfect for the job."

"Your brother has a serious case of wanderlust. I don't think he's ever going to ease up on his jet-setting ways. Jonathan is just like his father. Although, I never thought Phillip would marry and yet he gave me two amazing grandchildren."

Imani raised her shoulders. "Jonathan already travels back and forth between here and Dubai. He can attend meetings here using videoconferencing. It's not like it was in your day. And maybe one day, he'll settle down, maybe start a family, like Dad."

Her grandfather made one last attempt to plead his case. "To run my business, you need the right balance of heart and cunning. Both of which you already possess, my darling granddaughter. I just had to nurture it, and with you at the helm, I know our business will last for generations." He grimaced. "I can't have all that I took my lifetime building squandered or divvied up and sold to the highest bidders. Or, worse, I don't want your mother or grandmother to ever have to worry about finances. Only family will make sure of that."

The concern in his tone almost made her rethink her position. "Okay. Talk to Jonathan. See if he will run the day-to-day after you retire and I can have the final vote. I believe that is a fair compromise."

"Alright, that's doable." He took her hand in his and they resumed their walk. "I've set up a trust for Colt so he will never have to worry about his future."

"Thank you, Grandpa. Nash did as well. My child is already a millionaire, and he isn't even seven days old."

She didn't add that Colt would be the chief beneficiary of Lullababies, if she kept her company.

"Yep. Colt Porter Fortune is one blessed child." Grandpa kissed her cheek. "In more ways than one." He cocked his head. "Having both parents in his life will be an even bigger blessing." That was a not-so-subtle way of inquiring about the status of her relationship with Nash.

"I know I didn't go about this the traditional way, Grandpa, but Nash and I are both committed to co-parenting."

His eyebrows rose. "I guess that's the in thing now with you young people. Back in my day, we would have been Mr. and Mrs. before the baby's birth."

"And back in your day, people stayed married through misery. Thirty, forty years spent despising each other all for the children's sake." She pursed her lips. "Won't be me. The person I marry will want to be with me for always. Or, I'll remain single. I won't subject my son to a toxic environment."

"That's a good point," he said. "I never looked at it like that. Lucky for me, Zuri and I are in love. Every day I get up happy to see her face."

"Aww." Imani touched her chest. "I hope to get the same."

His cell phone vibrated with a message that made him look down. She was willing to bet it was her grandmother, judging by that huge smile across his face. After typing a response, Hammond said, "Nash seemed smitten with you when I met him."

"Well, I'll rely on your verdict about Nash's level of smitten-ness when you see him again today." She looked at her watch and hurried her steps. "It's time for me to nurse and Nash should be back from the ranch by now."

Her grandmother strolled toward them. She had on a sweatsuit and sneakers. "There you are. I was wondering where you both got off to." Then, eyes peeled on her hubby, Zuri made her way over to Hammond.

"We'll be back in a few," Hammond called out, snatching his wife close. "We're going to catch the sunset on Nash's boat."

"Uh-huh. So that's what we're calling it these days." Both gave her unapologetic shrugs before heading to the dock arm in arm.

Imani swallowed the bit of hopeful envy. Man, she really hoped to have something enduring like her grandparents had. Speaking of endurance, her mind kept straying toward that kiss she and Nash had shared. It had been sensual torture, because she had a few weeks before she could engage in intercourse. But she had no regrets. Her lips tingled as she replayed that encounter in her mind—the heat in his eyes, the shock waves going through her body, the feel of his hands and that low growl in her ear.

It had been too much and not enough at the same time.

And, oh, she needed more.

Maybe tonight, they could steal a few minutes to themselves for part two. In the meantime, Imani would think about all the wicked things that firm mouth and demanding tongue would do to her. But when she entered the guesthouse, all those thoughts flew out of her head.

Nash was there.

Holding her wedding veil in one hand.

The unspoken question was evident in the knit of his eyebrows.

Everyone around him was silent. Her mother held Colt, panic in her eyes. "Nash was just asking about this gown, and who it belonged to…" her mother squeaked out. Abena's flustered tone increased Imani's discomfort. Why hadn't she tossed the jumpsuit in the trash? He must have seen it inside the shopping bag that she must have left in the nursery.

Well, sometimes the best response was no response. Or a clean exit while she gathered her frazzled thoughts. Breaking eye contact with the father of her child, and ignoring her hammering heart, Imani marched over to her mother and held out her hands. "I'm sure Colt is hungry. I've got to feed him."

As soon as her mother placed Colt in her arms, Imani took off for the bedroom. How on earth did that jumpsuit end up in the nursery? She vaguely remembered her mother and grandmother clearing her trunk, but then... Wait. She had been changing Colt and had told her mother to leave it by the closet, and she would get it later.

But, of course, she had forgotten.

And now, she had Nash almost breathing down her neck, striding after her. She ducked inside the room but before she could close the door, he stood by the doorjamb holding up the veil. "Care to explain?"

He had a frown on his face, but his tone was gentle.

That was the only reason she stepped aside to let him enter. After undoing her buttons, she got Colt situated to feed and then faced the only man she should have ever thought about marrying.

"It was for convenience," she admitted. Good grief. That wasn't the thing to say. Colt began to fuss so she latched him on again.

Nash's eyes narrowed. "What do you mean?"

"You told me you didn't want children and I didn't want Colt to grow up without a father's love."

"So you decided to get a substitute?" He sounded butt-hurt.

She rushed to explain. "I wouldn't call it that. I wasn't looking for a substitute dad for Colt, more like a..."

"Replacement?" he growled out.

Dang, that didn't sound good, either. It would be misleading for her to blame it on pregnancy hormones. Imani had capably run her company the entire term of her pregnancy.

"These past six months I lived like a hermit. I tried not to think about you. I spent hours listening to Taylor Swift to try to get you out of my system, all the while you were looking for someone to fill my shoes."

"Wait. You listen to *Taylor Swift*?"

"Uh, what does it matter?" he countered. "My life is the equivalent of a sad song."

"B-but I didn't go through with it. I c-couldn't marry a man I d-didn't love," she stammered, burping Colt and then changing his position to her other breast. "That's what counts in the long run."

"Fair enough." He bunched the delicate material in his fists. She really wanted to save the veil, as it had been hand-made and cost more than it should, but she knew this wasn't the time to point that out. "So who is the mystery man?"

Of course, he would want to know. "It was Simon. My friend from graduate school. Well, former friend."

"Si—" He paced the room. "*I knew* it. I told you when I met him that he had the hots for you. And why wouldn't he? You're attractive, way out of his league, obviously. But what man can resist your charms?"

"Excuse me?" Colt startled in her arms. "Sorry, little one." She rubbed his back to comfort him. Lowering her voice, she spoke through her teeth. "It was a business arrangement with a friend. Nothing more." The memory of the look of heated attraction in Simon's eyes made her squirm. Well, it was just friendship on her part. She blew out a breath of frustration. "But either way, it doesn't matter because I didn't marry the man. I ran out of the court-house before we could finish saying the vows."

Nash's mouth dropped. "You did what?"

"Yes, I hid in the bathroom and then as soon as the coast was clear, I was out of there."

Nash covered his mouth but a snort escaped. "I actually pity the man." The snort led to a full-on laughing fest. He bent over, clutching his stomach.

"Stop!" she said, feeling the giggles rising within. "It's not funny."

"It's like a scene out of a rom-com or one of those movies you used to make me watch."

Colt disengaged and she placed him on her shoulder to burp him again. To her surprise, Nash came over and took over the task. Within minutes, Colt released a healthy belch. Nash then offered to change his diaper. Her heart warmed. He was really trying.

"I love you, little man," he said, bending over to kiss Colt's forehead. Their son drifted off to sleep and Nash swaddled him, then placed him on his back in the bassinet. Imani bit on her lower lip to keep from commending him, but also, she didn't think he would want her watching his every single move. Even if she was.

Nash placed a hand on his hip and asked gruffly, "So were you going to tell me?"

Her stomach clenched. "Tell you what?"

"About Colt? Simon?" He flailed his hands. "All of it."

She bit her lower lip again and shook her head. "I…" Imani trailed off. Her eyes misted. "I was going to tell you about Simon."

"Good."

"But if I hadn't gone into labor and you weren't my rescuer, I honestly don't know when I would have told you about Colt."

Nash nodded and then stalked out of the room. Imani grabbed the baby monitor and dashed after him as he uttered a curt goodbye to her family and raced out of the guesthouse. After begging her mother to keep an eye on Colt, Imani knew she couldn't let the night end this way. "Nash," she called out. He kept moving, cutting across the lawn to get into his house. "Wait! I need you to—" In her haste, she twisted her foot on a pebble and screeched, her butt hitting the soft earth beneath her.

In a flash, he was by her side, helping her to stand. When she cried out, he swung her up in his powerful arms. Nash turned to return her to the guesthouse, but she insisted they go to his place instead. After a moment's hesitation, he changed direction.

When he turned on the interior lights, Imani gasped at the cathedral ceiling, the wide-open space and the wall of windows that faced the deck. "This place is gorgeous."

He grunted what sounded like a thank-you before setting her back down on her feet, but she couldn't be sure. Time to get back to the topic on hand. She placed the baby monitor on the foyer entrance table, right beside a white envelope with what appeared to be a wedding invitation on top. The baby monitor fell, causing the invite to fall onto the floor.

"Sorry about that," she said and stooped to pick it up.

Nash rushed over to take it out of her hand. "Oh, I forgot about that. It's a wedding invitation for the end of January…" He trailed off. "But get this, I don't even know who the bride and groom will be. It's all pretty weird. My brothers and sisters received the same one, and maybe that's the only reason I haven't thrown it away." He shook his head before dropping the envelope on the table.

"Oh…" Imani wasn't sure what else to say so she back-tracked to the previous, pressing conversation. Twisting her fingers, she shuffled from one foot to the next and continued. "I'm sorry you're mad at me but this isn't all on me," she said in a gentle tone.

"I'm not mad at you," he groaned, jabbing a finger in his chest. "I'm mad at *me*. None of this would have happened if I weren't such a…coward." He deflated. "I pushed away the best thing to happen to me because I was afraid."

Her heart squeezed. "What you're feeling is understandable. And if we dwell on the what-ifs and should-haves, we won't move forward." Her shoulders sagged. "And that's what I want to do, Nash. Move past all this."

"I'm not good at that. I keep allowing my past to dictate my actions in the present. Like my relationship with my father." He rubbed his head. "But I know I must." His voice cracked. "Because now that I have you back in my life, I know I can't let you go. And now that I have a son, I can never *not* be his father. No matter where I go in the world, I can't run from that. And though I'm not gonna lie, I'm scared as all get-out, I don't want to.

Imani folded her arms and arched an eyebrow. "So don't."

She didn't know who made the first move, but the next thing she knew they were hugging, kissing and touching. Trying to assuage a six-month hunger from which there could only be one relief.

With a savage growl, he crushed his lips to hers. She moaned, long and loud, welcoming his hands exploring the top half of her body, appreciating his mindfulness that she had just had a baby.

The friction, the fire, threatened to consume her. Nash's tongue explored where his hands had been, an enticing substitute. Her knees buckled, and he came down with her, his arms a steady brace. It was the feel of the cool marble on her back that made her senses return.

"Nash, I can't…" His lips found the base of her neck.

"There's many things I can do," he said, his voice a rumble, his teeth grazing her earlobes. He wasn't playing fair.

"I want to, but we've got to get back. Colt won't sleep for more than twenty minutes max. Plus, I have a house full of family waiting on me, clamoring to see how this all plays out. I can't have them barging up here to—" she made air quotes "'—help resolve our dispute.'" After pressing her hands against his shoulders, she stood and rebuttoned the top of her dress.

"I understand." Nash got to his feet, too, then whispered, "I miss you. I've missed you and I will be missing you even more tonight."

"Same." She picked up the baby monitor. Colt was still asleep. Good. She splayed her hands on his chest. "How about you give me a quick tour before we return to my welcome party?"

"Alright. There's one place in particular I'd like to show you." He waggled his brows.

Imani rolled her eyes. "Let me get the clearance from the doctor first and then we can revisit that possibility."

"Okay, it's a date."

She teased, "But it will be hard for you to top the private plane ride to New York City so we could see a Broadway show, especially with a baby in tow."

"I'll think of something." Nash led the way to the spacious kitchen. As expected, he had top-of-the-line appliances and the decor was a mix of modern and rustic. She drooled over the glass-door refrigerator, which appeared to be stocked with the bare minimum. Not that she commented. She had a similar situation at her home in Cactus Grove.

His master suite was on the same floor and there were three other bedrooms on the second floor, each with their own bathrooms. From his bedroom, there was a walkout that provided an impressive scenic view.

Her new-mother eye detected his place would need serious toddler-proofing when that time came. *Hold up.* Just because Nash still desired her and had voluntarily changed a diaper, it didn't mean he was in it for a lifetime. Because as her mother told her, parenting was a never-ending commitment and it wouldn't get easier with age. The older they got, the bigger the problems. Imani touched her abdomen. She didn't even know if *she* was ready for what was to come. But at least she knew she wanted motherhood.

She sauntered outside, enjoying the gentle night breeze, the night sounds and the tranquility. The fresh fall air cleared her mind.

Nash was still quite a few steps behind her in embracing parenthood. She had to allow him time to catch up, so she couldn't complicate that process by allowing him into her bed. No matter how much she wanted to.

He came to stand behind her, wrapping his arms about her waist. The scent of his cologne served as an aphrodisiac. "Guess what I have in my garage?"

She paused before turning in his arms. "You didn't?" There was only one vehicle she knew of that would put that sparkle in his eyes and excitement in his voice. "You *did*?" she squealed, and did a little jig.

"I sure did." He grinned, hand extended. "Care for a five-minute ride?"

"Five minutes?"

His voice dropped. "There's a lot we can do in five minutes."

Well, okay then. She sure was game to find out.

Chapter Ten

Fifteen minutes. That's how long they had been gone from the guesthouse.

Nash had kept a close eye on the time. Now, he turned on the light in the garage, appreciating Imani's harsh intake of breath. The dark green color of the Jaguar sparkled under the showcase lights he had had specially installed.

"She is a beauty," she said, and whistled, running her free hand on the hood. The other clutched the baby monitor. He made a mental note to install the app on her phone, as he had done with his. "What do you call her?"

"I haven't named her."

Imani placed a hand on her hips. "She is a horse on wheels. She needs to have a name."

"Good point. Okay, I'll think of one." Nash opened the car door for her and waited until she was settled before jogging around to the driver's side and starting up the Jaguar. Then he pressed the garage-door opener and crept outside, taking in the night sounds. Once he had backed out, he put on the old Rascal Flatts hit "Life Is a Highway."

"When this song ends that's our cue to end this joyride. Deal?" he said.

They bumped fists. "Deal." Nash hit the gas, loving the perks of living on a private compound. Imani squealed, raising her hands in the air. "Whoa. Go, baby, go!"

And go, he did. In a matter of seconds, they were at 100 miles per hour. It felt smooth, like butter…like velvet, eating up the gravel, flying past the fields, the fall colors a satisfying blur. He glanced at the beautiful woman next to him and smiled. This was what he had been waiting on. Imani by his side in his restored ride. With the window down, her hair blew in the wind. He dipped the curve, enjoying her whoop of delight, and headed toward the entrance. He'd stop beneath the awning.

He snapped to attention and hit the steering wheel. "That's it!"

"That's what?" she asked.

"I'm calling her Velvet."

"Ooh." Imani gyrated her hips. "I like it." She rubbed the plush leather. "Velvet, you're giving me quite a ride tonight."

"This is just like old times," Nash murmured, expecting her to laugh in return. But she sobered, sinking back into her seat. He slowed and turned down the music. "What's wrong?"

"You know we can never go back, don't you?" she asked, her hands folded in her lap.

He shook his head in confusion. "Go back to what?"

"Our lives are forever changed because of Colt and I'm not looking to relive—" she did her second air quotes for the night "'—old times.'" She gestured her hands between them. "We have a son to think of."

Nash cringed. "Listen, I meant we were having fun like we always do. I have been in a funk these past few months and this is the first time in a long time, I am enjoying the company of a fine woman—a woman I have strong feelings for—and it feels good to feel that way again. I'm not going to apologize for that and I'm not going to regret it, either." He executed a U-turn, the air tense between them.

After a few beats, she mumbled, "I'm sorry if I ruined the vibe or misjudged you."

"Thank you for apologizing. Your assumption ruined this vibe and you did misjudge me. I still plan on having loads of fun with you…and Colt. Just being around you is fun for me. That's not going to change because we're parents."

They finished the rest of the way in silence and he entered the garage in a way different mood from when he had left. The song ended. Neither moved.

"I'm sorry, again. I propose a do-over." She sniffled. "I'm just worried about you forgetting about Colt. It's easy to get caught up and…" She trailed off and murmured, "Never mind, it's hard to explain and I'm feeling like the big, bad monster who shackled you with a baby you didn't want." She opened the door and made a move to get out.

Nash held her arm. "Baby, you really think I would forget, or rather, *want* to forget my son?" The fact that he had to ask this question crushed him.

"Not on purpose," she whispered, her head dipped to her chest.

"Yes, Colt has changed my life, and yes, I am processing and dealing with that right along with my fears. But you didn't shackle me with anything, to use your words, and I'm glad that he's here." His words jarred him into realizing he had spoken nothing but the truth.

"You are?" she said, her voice quavering with relief.

His chest tightened. Goodness, Imani really believed that he resented Colt's presence, that he saw his son as an intrusion in his life. No wonder she had reacted the way she had a couple of minutes ago. "Yes, I'm glad that Colt is here. I'm glad he has all his fingers and toes. I'm glad at everything he does. I love him. I'm not just saying that, Imani. I love my child."

Imani gave him a bright smile, and her eyes welled up. "I'm glad…and relieved."

"Good." Nash opened the door and once again reached for her hand. He craved any kind of physical contact with her. "Now, let's go check on our son." When they made their way back, he went out of his way to follow up his words with actions. He remained glued to Colt's side for the rest of the night, making sure to tell Colt he loved him.

Before her family left, they gave him kisses and hugs, praising him for a job well done. But if he was being completely honest, he was exhausted.

And that exhaustion grew throughout the next week and a half. Being a daddy was the hardest and most demanding job he had ever had. He barely slept, helping with diaper changes, feedings, baths and bedtime. Repeat, repeat, repeat. But Nash was not about to voice that aloud.

Nope.

His mother and siblings had called to offer help but Nash had declined.

He wasn't going to chance Imani thinking he wasn't committed, or was foisting his responsibility on to someone else. Because he was committed. He just wasn't able to think coherently and he had a meeting coming up that he needed to prepare for, but any free moment was spent taking power naps because Nash had given up on ever catching up on sleep.

Sleep? Who needed it?

If he stopped moving, he would pass out and he wouldn't wake up for days. Imani was just as tired as he was, yet she kept at it. And so would he.

So they stayed on the grind, in an unspoken face-off, like Energizer Bunnies, making Colt their only priority, providing round-the-clock care. The same thing, day in, day out. Imani even took a step back from being involved with the expansion of Lullababies. He knew for a fact that most of the time when Nia called, Imani would find an excuse to end the conversation.

But then, Ridge called early that morning to inform Nash about an emergency on the ranch. Nash insisted on going in to the office to investigate. Not even to himself would he admit that it was because he sought a much-needed break. And if he avoided meeting Imani's eyes when he told her he had to head into work, and thus, potentially miss Colt's first doctor's appointment, though his mother was on her way to assist, it had nothing to do with guilt. Nothing at all. At least that's what he told himself as he got dressed and headed out of the house, his steps light. Was it him? Or did the air feel sharper and the sun seem brighter this morning? He marched toward the Range Rover loving the crunch of the autumn leaves under his boots. Jumping into his Range Rover, Nash took off, leaving nothing but dust in his wake.

Since he hadn't eaten breakfast, he decided to stop by the Daily Grind to get a cup of coffee. The coffee shop was once a one-story modest home that had been converted to a restaurant in the 1930s. Situated across the road from the feed store made it an ideal location for ranchers to stop in for coffee and sweet treats.

After parking out front, Nash traipsed across the wide front porch and opened the door. The bell chimed when he entered and he greeted the workers. The place wasn't fancy but it was cute and bright, with red gingham curtains. There were about a dozen small wooden tables, as well as a counter along the back with stools. The Daily Grind was a hang out spot for the locals to engage in local gossip, and Nash always felt right at home.

While he waited for his order, Nash noticed a queue at one of the tables and beelined over to investigate. To his surprise, Beau Weatherly sat there with his Free Life Advice plaque posted. Beau was a retired ranch investor who had lost his wife about five years ago. The man was a big contributor and had brought in many initiatives to Chatelaine. He was loved and respected by the community. Nash had heard about Beau giving out advice every morning from 7:00 to 8:30 a.m. from his siblings, but this was the first time he had seen Beau "open for business."

Nash's order came up. After tipping the waitstaff, Nash took a hearty sip of his Americano and then decided to join Beau's line.

Once it was his turn, he slipped into the seat and got right to it. "If a man had a terrible role model for being a father, can he still be a good father to his own child if he works at it?" His face heated at his question. Maybe it was too deep for the kind of advice the distinguished gentleman usually doled out.

Beau took Nash's hand in both of his and looked straight at him. "Absolutely. You determine who you are—no one and nothing else." Nash thanked the older man, then stood. He hadn't expected Beau to say otherwise but his spirits lifted at those words.

A few minutes later, Nash pulled up to his designated parking spot at the ranch offices near the main house, with the gusto of a bear coming out of hibernation. There was a whole other world going on while he had been sequestered in the guesthouse with Imani and Colt.

There were a few other parking spaces in front of the building for guests and more in the back of the ranch for employees. Nash pulled open the door of the building, then wiped his boots on the welcome mat and entered the small reception area. He tipped his hat at Maria, the part-time receptionist who helped with basic clerical duties such as filing, handling emailing and other duties as assigned.

"Arlo is waiting for you in your office," Maria offered, once he had shared the perfunctory baby pictures. He passed Sabrina's and Jade's offices before rapping on the last door at the end of the hallway.

"Come in," Arlo said. Ridge was also inside and seated on one of two chairs on the other side of the desk.

Nash squelched his surprise at how comfortable Ridge looked behind his desk. He paused. "Am I about to lose my job?" he asked, only half-joking. His heart thumped in his chest.

Ridge gestured him inside, his tone solemn. "Hey, bro. Come sit down. You need to see this." A sense of dread lined Nash's stomach. Both men had grave looks on their faces.

That's when Nash zoned in on the photos spread across the desk. He gasped and shot his brothers a glance. "This can't be real."

"It is."

Nash dropped into the chair. A chill ran up his body. If what he was seeing is true, that meant someone was purposely sabotaging their business, and unless they found the perpetrator, the Fortune family plans for the ranch would come to a screeching halt. He could almost hear Casper laughing from beyond the grave.

Chapter Eleven

All the photos that she'd seen of happy mothers, pushing their happy infants in the strollers, were nothing but lies. For her, motherhood was like a Jenga game and it only needed one small error for everything to fall apart. Imani stood in her driveway with the passenger door ajar, her mouth open in shock.

After Nash had bolted out the door early that morning, Imani had swallowed her resentment. It must be really nice to be able to drive away without a backward glance, but she wasn't about to call him and get on his case about it. If he didn't want to be there, she wasn't going to force him. And, no, she hadn't bought his thin excuse that he was needed at the ranch, when she had heard his brother tell him that they could meet virtually.

Frankly, Imani was too tired to argue.

Her bones ached from trying to survive on roughly three hours sleep. Colt needed to be fed every hour, sometimes less. She fretted that he wasn't getting enough but she wasn't sure.

Her pride gave her the wind she needed to get Colt ready for his doctor's appointment but she had run out of time to tame her unkempt hair. Honestly, she didn't have the energy to care. Stifling a moan, she had donned a wrinkled long-sleeved T-shirt and a pair of stained black jeans.

But just as she placed Colt into his car seat, she noticed he had soiled his clothes, the refuse seeping out, while he just stared at her.

"Why couldn't you have done this five minutes ago?" She grunted, dropping the baby bag at her feet. Imani hated being late and this mishap was going to set her back by at least twenty minutes. Colt's response was to burst into a full-fledged wail.

Her shoulders shook as she began to weep right along with her baby boy. "H-hang on. I'm going to h-help you. Just as s-soon as I g-get my-myself together." This was ridiculous. She had experience running a million-dollar company and she couldn't handle a week-old baby?

A hand on her shoulder made her jump. "How can I help?" Wendy asked, slipping an arm around her shoulders. Those soft-spoken words were her undoing. She had been too distraught to register the other woman pulling up in the golf cart. Leaning into the embrace, Imani fell apart. Wendy rocked her while she cried. Eventually, with gentle prodding, Imani was able to explain the problem. "There now, I'm pretty sure the pediatrician will understand if you're running behind schedule. You're a new mom and these things happen. Now, why don't you call the office and let them know what's going on and I will get Colt cleaned up?"

Imani exhaled and nodded.

In a flash, Wendy was heading back into the house with the crying infant, with Imani trailing behind. The guesthouse was a mess—there were diapers, baby clothes, empty food cartons littered throughout the living room and kitchen—but she was too exhausted to be embarrassed.

Imani plopped into the couch and called the doctor. The receptionist pushed the time back to later that afternoon. Imani set her alarm in her phone so she wouldn't forget.

She could hear Wendy singing and talking to Colt while the bathwater ran. Dropping her phone in her purse, she sunk farther into the cushions and closed her eyes.

The next thing she knew, Wendy was giving her a gentle shake. "I'm sorry to wake you, but Colt's hungry and I didn't see any milk in the fridge."

"I didn't get a chance to pump this morning. Honestly, I've been breastfeeding more than I've given him bottles." Not that she was able to produce more than an ounce or two. Imani thought her milk would be gushing like the videos she had seen on pumping. She made a move to stand.

Tucking the baby under her arm, Wendy waved for her to sit. "You can pump later. Right now, let's get him fed and then we will be on our way."

"They gave me an afternoon appointment instead." Dang, she could barely keep her eyes open. That mininap was a tease.

"Awesome. So after you've nursed, you're going to go into your bedroom and get some more rest. I'll take care of Colt." She looked around the space, taking in the disarray. Imani opened her mouth to apologize but Wendy lifted a hand. "I'm going to start cleaning up while you feed your son. No need to explain. I have been there."

Grateful tears slid down Imani's face. She choked out a thank-you and fed Colt. Within minutes, he was asleep. Poor little guy. Colt hadn't slept well the night before. To Imani, he seemed hungry all the time and she didn't know what to do to help him. Oh, goodness. What if she wasn't able to provide milk for her child?

Imani rubbed his little cheek and gave him a kiss before placing him in his bassinet. She did a quick pump, praying for a heavier flow, ending up with a couple ounces this time. Whew. Imani put the two bottles of milk in the refrigerator. Wendy was in the laundry room adjacent to the kitchen, humming some tune.

She shuffled into the bedroom to get some shut-eye. When she awakened three hours later at 1:00 p.m., she popped out of bed. She couldn't believe she had slept that long. Imani headed into the living room, eager to see her son. Then she stopped.

The guesthouse was immaculate. Everything shone. And the smell of lemons filled her nostrils.

Wendy and Jade sat on the couch and both women gave her a smile. Colt was awake on his aunt's lap, pumping his legs.

"Oh, my goodness," Imani said, dabbing at her eyes. "Thank you so much for cleaning and for watching Colt." She lowered her eyes, wishing they hadn't had to tidy up for her, but she was doing the best she could considering the circumstances. Imani changed the subject. "I feel refreshed after that nap."

"It was our pleasure," Wendy said, coming to give her a hug. "We were glad to help. Colt's laundry is finished and folded and his tummy is full."

"Plus, I had fun playing with my nephew," Jade said, taking in Imani's getup. Her sister-in-law wore jeans, boots and a colorful blouse, and she looked lovely. And clean.

"Nash texted that he should be back in time to take you to Colt's appointment," Wendy offered, breaking into her thoughts.

Imani folded her lips into her mouth to keep from uttering something surly about him. Instead, she planted a smile on her face and muttered, "That's fine." Her phone alarm went off and she went to retrieve it out of her purse, which Wendy must have moved to the coffee table.

She gave her curls a futile pat and looked at her watch.

Maybe she could squeeze in a shower and wash her hair…
"If you don't mind hanging around a little longer, I'll
freshen up a bit. Get some me time before our appointment at three thirty." As soon as she said those words, she
chided herself. She should be all about her son. Right now,
she sounded selfish.

"Take all the time you need," Jade said. "We ordered
pizza and Nash is picking it up on his way back."

"And don't you dare feel guilty about taking time for
yourself." Wendy wagged a finger. "Self-care is important
for your mental health and overall well-being."

"Duly noted," Imani said, before excusing herself. How
her life had changed in such a short time! She had under-
estimated just how much but it would be good to feel like
herself again.

"I can't believe he grew an inch already," Nash said
when they left the pediatrician's office later that afternoon.
Wendy had ventured with them to the doctor's office while
Jade had left right after Nash came. Nash was now on his
way back home, but he was dropping off his mother first.

"And I can't believe he's only gained a couple of ounces,"
Imani replied, disheartened, her tone tinged with frost. She
cupped her abdomen. Disappointment in herself as a mom
weighed her down. Plus, she was still low-key ticked off at
Nash for his brash exit that morning but since his mother
was around, she held her tongue. Imani didn't want Wendy
viewing her as churlish, especially since Nash's mom had
been lovely and supportive during the appointment. Watching Colt get his first shots had been traumatic for her and
so it was good that Wendy had been there to keep her calm.

She had gritted her teeth, when Nash cooed, "Come on,
little man, be a tough guy" over and over. It had taken an

enormous amount of restraint to keep from snapping that Colt was just a baby.

Wendy reached over from the passenger seat to pat her shoulder. "He'll put on some weight soon." Imani gave her a slight smile before turning her head to look out the window.

When the doctor said that Colt needed to gain a few pounds, she had held her breath to keep from breaking down. All the long hours and sleepless nights had been for naught. She was failing at motherhood. And she couldn't blame Nash for this because she was Colt's sole nutrition supply. The doctor had suggested she consult with a lactation specialist and supplement with formula, because she might not be making enough milk.

She, Imani, who had been high-school salutatorian, maintained a 4.0 in college and had launched a successful retail chain, couldn't produce enough milk, a couple of ounces actually, to sustain a newborn.

This was beyond mortifying.

"Yeah, that doctor doesn't know what he's talking about," Nash added, giving her hand a squeeze.

Imani rolled her eyes. She knew he was trying to be encouraging but she just wasn't in the mood.

Nash pulled up to the main house. Wendy asked if they wanted to come inside and offered to give Imani a tour. Plus, she had made a hearty bowl of chili and corn bread. Imani's stomach growled. But Nash was already shaking his head.

"Can we take a rain check?" he asked. "There's a lot going on at the ranch and I've got to get to the bottom of it."

"Okay, call me later and let me know what's going on," Wendy said.

"I will. If I figure it out."

Ugh. That meant Nash was going to be busy tonight, leaving her to deal with Colt on her own. The fact that he didn't have to because his brothers would handle whatever it was irked her to another level.

Throwing them a kiss, Wendy exited and strutted inside her home.

Imani turned to check on Colt, avoiding meeting Nash's eyes.

She sure was cross with Nash. Maybe her grumpy disposition was because he had the nerve to look fine and rested while she felt worn-out and drained. Even though she had washed her hair and donned a cute brown ribbed dress, she could see her face looked gaunt and her eyes had dark circles under them, plus her nails were cracked and her feet sore. But she needed to take care of Colt and make sure he gained weight by the next appointment.

And if it meant she was going to lose more sleep to make it happen, well, that's what she would do.

Chapter Twelve

He was getting the silent treatment. And he deserved every bit of it. Imani hadn't fussed or argued, but her displeasure hit him like a tsunami. She hadn't even asked what was going on at the ranch. And she hadn't allowed him to do anything for Colt since he had gotten home.

Sitting on the rocker in the nursery with his laptop on his lap, Nash regretted leaving her in the lurch that morning. But he hadn't anticipated that he would be facing such a big crisis at work, or that he would really want to talk to Imani about it.

Only, she wouldn't even look him in the eyes.

Just then, the door creaked and Imani sauntered in, holding a laundry basket. Colt must be asleep in the next room. She opened the drawers and began placing the clothes inside. She was dressed in her pajamas, which said, *Colt's Mom.* He figured it was a specialty item from her store. Colt was one of the most well-dressed babies he had ever seen. He had a plethora of coordinated monogrammed onesies, blankets and bibs.

"Do you need any help?" he asked, placing his laptop aside, already knowing what the answer would be.

"Nope."

He exhaled. "Ugh. This is ridiculous."

She swung around, eyes blazing, and placed a hand on

her hip. "*Ridiculous?* Really? Is that what we're calling your juvenile actions?"

Nash stood and walked over to her. "I'm the foreman. If something is wrong, I have to—"

She wagged a finger, interrupting him. "Don't even utter the rest of that exaggeration. You didn't have to do anything this morning. You chose to go because you didn't want to be here with me and Colt." Her voice hitched. "You would rather be anywhere than here. So all that talk about wanting to be a father to Colt was just talk."

Nash could hear the hurt in her voice and his shoulders sagged. "I want to be here helping you and I want to give Colt my best, but I just need…balance. It doesn't mean that I don't care."

Tears streaked down her face. "Well, you could have fooled me. I don't get to pick up and run off when things get tough. That's not what you do when you love someone. You don't…leave."

Her words pierced his chest. Is that how she saw him?

Their breakup was on him but he didn't see it as running away. He saw it as being upfront about how he felt at the time. Colt's arrival changed all that, but Nash refused to feel guilty about trying to insert normalcy into his life. She needed to do the same.

"You're behaving like parenting has shackles. You stay cooped up in here twenty-four hours a day. The only reason why you left the house was because Colt had a doctor's appointment. This isn't healthy."

To his surprise, Imani sunk into the rocker and wept. "You're right. I—I'm sorry for coming at you like that." She looked up at him and the fear in her eyes made his stomach clench. "I'm scared of going outside and Colt getting sick. I'm scared to leave him alone too long." She flailed her hands. "I'm just scared of everything. But most of all, I'm scared Colt is going to starve because I'm not feeding him enough." She broke into a heavy sob.

Nash got to his feet and hugged her close, allowing her to get a good cry in. He kissed the top of her head. "Oh, baby, you're doing way more than enough. In fact, you're going overboard. We are here acting like zombies when the solution is right in the kitchen cabinet."

She wiped her face and furrowed her brow. "What do you mean?"

"Come with me." He took her hand, led her into the kitchen and turned on the light. She slipped into the chair at the kitchen table. Then he opened the cupboard and took out a metal can.

Her reddened eyes went wide. "You took out a can of formula?"

"Yes. We need to use it."

She cocked her head. "Every book I've read on raising babies says breast is best."

"And where's that getting you? Neither you nor Colt has gotten a good night's sleep in days."

"I'm not doing it." She lifted her chin. "I'm not about to score a one on the motherhood scale."

"Motherhood scale?" He shook his head. "What on earth are you talking about? You're in competition with yourself. You know that, right? You're already the most amazing person in the world as far as Colt is concerned. You are the number-one voice he wants to hear, the number-one face he wants to see."

On cue, Colt began to wail.

She looked upward and groaned. "I just fed him twenty minutes ago. Why is he up?" Her lower lip trembled. She made a move to stand, but he placed a hand on her shoulder. "Sit."

Colt's cries got a little louder.

"Let me just go get him," Imani said, her butt half out of the chair.

"No, you need to rest," he said gently. "Colt will be alright for a few minutes while we talk. Besides, his lungs could use the workout and it's not like there are neighbors close by to hear him." Nash lifted her chin with his index finger. "It's wise to accept assistance when it's needed. Please quit punishing yourself for not producing enough breast milk. Love means doing what's best for him, not for you. What's important is that Colt is getting what he needs."

Her eyes misted as he continued. "I'm giving you permission to be human. You don't have to be a superwoman. You don't have to be perfect at everything. And, it's alright to take a break. Let me help you and our son."

"Okay." She took her seat.

A small win. Whew. "Great." He massaged his neck. "So, how about we try him with the formula? What do you say?" For several heart pounding seconds, he watched the varying expressions play across her face.

Then she tucked her lips into her mouth and nodded.

Nash pulled the tab on the metal container. It made a satisfying rip in the otherwise quiet of the night. He took out the baby-formula mixer, plugged it in and then poured the right amount of water and formula as directed. He turned on the mixer, loving the whirr. Secretly, Nash had been waiting to use this gadget that many parents had said was a must-have.

He peered over to Imani. She gripped the chair, her knuckles white. He knew the decision wasn't easy and prayed the benefits would outweigh any guilt she might feel.

Nash quickened his movements before she caved. Judging by those escalated cries, their son was impatient, a characteristic he shared with both his parents. He hurriedly got one of the baby bottles that his mother had sterilized and stored. Setting the dial on the mixer to two ounces, he placed the bottle under the spout and pressed the switch, appreciating the gurgle as warm formula poured out.

"Okay, I'm ready," he said.

Imani bolted out of the chair and scuttled into the room, coming back with Colt in her arms. Nash gestured for her to hand him over and then slipped the bottle inside that tiny mouth. Colt's mouth opened and closed as he tried to assimilate to the new bottle.

Poor little guy was frustrated that he couldn't latch on, his mouth seeking. Imani hovered close. "Let me try."

Nash did as she asked and wiped his brow. "That wasn't as easy as I imagined."

"It never is."

They shared a laugh at her dry response. Their first laugh in days. His chest lightened. Returning to her seat, Imani plopped the bottle in Colt's mouth and he began to feed, guzzling down the contents with speed.

"Wow. How did you do that?"

"I have no idea." She eyed the bundle in her hands. "Look at him go." She gave Nash a beaming smile, her lashes thickening with unshed tears. Her curls rested on her shoulders, framing her face just so, and his heart skipped a beat. She looked beautiful. "I have to admit he's pretty impressive."

"I agree. He had to have had an ounce already." Nash's chest puffed. "He's a champion."

Imani pulled out the bottle to burp Colt, who immediately started to fuss. "Hang on. I'll give you back your bottle in a minute." Of course, then he burped, so she gave him the rest. Soon Colt was fast asleep, leaving a small remnant of milk at the bottom of the bottle.

Gratitude flooded through Nash at his son's satisfied expression. A small niggle of doubt at his own incompetence teased his mind but he was too happy at the progress they had made tonight to dwell on it.

"If that snore is any indication, I think he'll be out for a while," Imani said, relief etched on her face.

"I'm counting on it." He gave her a pointed look. "You need a break."

"You're right."

"And admitting that doesn't make you a bad mother. It makes you a wise one. You don't want to burn out and become impatient and overwhelmed." He knew that admission had been difficult for her. "I'll make sure you get a break. How about a spa day soon?"

She closed her eyes briefly. "That sounds heavenly."

"I'm on it."

"I'm going to put the baby down and then you can tell me all about what's going on at the ranch," Imani whispered and walked toward the nursery. "Let's see how he does in here tonight." Nash rushed to get the bassinet out of the master bedroom and hauled it into the nursery, setting it next to the changing table. He made sure to turn on the baby monitor, then he grabbed his laptop.

Side by side, Nash and Imani rested the infant inside. Colt didn't even budge. Nash couldn't resist taking a picture.

They made their way to the living room. "You did good, Daddy," Imani said, sitting and tucking her legs beneath her. She had no idea how those words served as a balm for his unease.

"Let's see if he sleeps for an extended time."

Imani rubbed her eyes. "I hope so. He needs it."

"So do you." Nash went behind her on the couch and massaged her shoulders. He kneaded her back muscles, making sure to work out the knots in her neck. His baby was tense.

Tilting her head back, she groaned. "That feels so good."

Lowering his head, Nash cradled her head between his palms and placed a tender kiss on her lips. "I can't wait until I can use my lips. I'm going to kiss every delectable inch of your body."

He heard a sharp intake of breath. "I'm going to hold you to that." Imani patted the space next to her and he went by her side. "Now, get to talking…"

Nash opened up his laptop. "I met with Ridge and Arlo. Someone cut a few of our metal fences and opened some of our livestock cages."

Imani gasped. "Say what?"

"We were able to find and rescue most of the animals, and fortunately, none were hurt." He tapped the screen. "That's why I have been reviewing the recordings over the past couple days to see if we can find the person or persons responsible."

"Oh, no. It sounds like someone is trying to sabotage the ranch." She scooted forward, her brow furrowed. "Did you call the cops?"

"Yes, two deputies came by and questioned our workers. They said they plan to launch an investigation. But they didn't have faith that the culprits would be caught. They speculate it could have been day-labor workers, who would now be long gone. None of the other ranches have reported any strange incidents. Frankly, the cops were shocked to hear about this happening on this side of town." He scoffed. "According to them, nothing generally happens in Chatelaine."

"Honestly, I'm floored," Imani said. "This is a small town where everyone seems to know everyone. Are you sure these local cops are trained to conduct a wide-range investigation?"

"Honestly? I don't know. But I convinced them to allow us to do our own investigation as well, make the guilty party think they've gotten away with it. I want to catch them in the act. So I'm not just reviewing past footage, but daily footage as well."

Her eyes were filled with empathy. "I'm just glad no harm came to the animals. Is there something I can do?"

"No, I've been going through hours and hours of recordings from our security system for the past couple days or so. Our holdings are large, and luckily, we had just installed security cameras at different angles. But that's another reason why it's taking a while to go through." He rubbed his eyes. The work was tedious and, yes, they could more than afford to hire their own investigators, but Nash needed to help. He was foreman and responsible for the safety of the people and animals on the ranch. "I'll take my time and go through the footage, and you've got your own business to run," he reminded her.

"Yes, well, I'm toying with the idea of selling my shares of the company to Nia." She pulled on her pajama top and didn't meet his eyes.

His mouth dropped. "Why would you do that?"

"I don't want to miss out on anything with Colt. I can't. My father is wonderful, but he was and is a part-time father. Now, when he's here, he is the absolute best. But he isn't always here." She ticked off her points with her index finger. "Dad missed recitals, and tennis matches and school performances." She dabbed at her eyes. "I can't do the same to Colt. I want to be in his life full-time. That's also the reason why I couldn't assume full responsibility for my grandfather's company when he retires. I'm hoping Jonathan will agree to take over the helm stateside when that time comes, though I offered to be the final vote when needed."

"I understand where you're coming from, but you can make a conscious choice not to make the same mistake your father did." She raised her eyebrows at him. He lifted a hand. "I know. I know. Pot. Kettle. I need to take my own advice. But look at your mother. Though she married into one of the wealthiest families in Texas, she kept working as a guidance counselor. Even now, your mom is involved in charities and all sorts of hobbies. And my mom raised six children and still did her own thing."

He ran a hand through his hair. "You're not looking at this from the right angle. You're the boss, Imani. You don't have to miss anything. It's called scheduling. And Colt won't be young all the time. The older he gets, the less he'll need you. Heck, as soon as I hit the fourth grade, I didn't want to be seen around my mother until I graduated high school. And the main reason I hung out with her on graduation day was because Jade had let it slip that Mom was getting us both cars as gifts."

"Oh, snap. I get it. I didn't want my mother around much, either." She appeared pensive, then admitted, "You're right."

"Of course, I'm right. Now, how about tomorrow morning, we get out of this house and get lattes at the Daily Grind? It's not as fancy as the LC Club, but they have the best caramel macchiato I've ever had."

She arched an eyebrow. "Hmm…you remembered my favorite coffee." Then she shrugged. "Alright, let's go. But it's cold outside. Colt might get sick."

He wasn't about to let her back out now. "We'll bundle him really good and we'll take him some formula in case he gets hungry." He watched her face fall at those words, but Imani didn't say anything, and he figured she was still grappling with her inability to nurse. In time, he hoped she would accept she didn't have to be perfect to be a great Mom.

"We'll go after the morning rush," she said.

"Deal. It's a date."

Sitting next to him on the couch, Imani expelled a long breath. Nash sounded so excited about their excursion that she didn't have the heart to turn him down. She was pretty sure he recalled that visiting coffee houses had been one of their many dates as a couple. Coffee and cupcakes. They typically spent hours talking and people-watching in the coffee shop. Nash gave her an expectant look. "Remember, I'm waiting on you to tell me when you want to do the spa visit."

"Yes. I'll reach out to Nia and see if she wants to come with me." Imani pulled out her phone. After a couple of texts back and forth, she asked Nash, "How about the fifteenth?"

"That could work. I have a meeting with my family in the morning, but the rest of the afternoon is wide open."

"Are you sure?" Nash sounded confident but he had never been alone with Colt before. Imani didn't know how she felt about that.

"Yes, I'll be okay." He didn't come off as sure this time, but she decided to take him at his word.

"Okay, but I'll be calling to check on you guys."

Nash slapped his jeans with his hands. "Now that all that's settled, if you were serious about helping me, I have hours of recording and I could use an extra eye."

"Okay, let me get my laptop. Let's meet up in the kitchen."

Imani scuttled into the bedroom, making sure to also grab the charger. She peeped in on Colt and he was still asleep. Putting on the Keurig, Imani made two cups of coffee, while Nash got them situated.

Then they watched reels and reels of recordings, even getting a few laughs in between. Who knew it could be fun watching silent videos, especially since they sped them up? It was even more hilarious when they made up possible conversations. But anything she did with Nash was fun, because it was Nash.

When she finally went to sleep that night, Nash Fortune filled her mind, her dreams. Imani thrashed about in bed, wanting and hoping he would join her. They couldn't have sex, but she craved the warmth of his hard body, how she used to snuggle against him and how he would draw her close to cuddle while they slept. Things a real couple did together that went beyond physical attraction. Things that bound one heart to another.

Pillow talk…

Playing footsies…

Intimacy.

But after the way things ended between them, Imani knew she couldn't put herself out there again. When she got the all clear, she would content herself with assuaging the physical need. Yes, she loved him, but she wouldn't become consumed with him. She would keep a small part of her heart in reserve. It was the only way she would be able to move on when their time here came to an end.

Chapter Thirteen

Colt refused to latch on. He scrunched his face and screamed before seeking… Seeking nourishment she didn't have. A bonding she couldn't provide.

Imani squeezed her eyes shut to keep from breaking into tears. When she had awakened that morning, her breasts had felt full and she'd taken that as a sign that her body was ready to continue doing what should be natural. Not to mention that the lactation specialist had called to ask how everything was going. When she conveyed her continued struggles with breastfeeding, the specialist had encouraged her not to give up, but also reassured her that she was doing the right thing by ensuring the baby got the proper nutrition through supplementing as needed.

Nevertheless, Imani had tried again. And again. Now, both her and her baby were frustrated. He stiffened, bunched his fists and wailed, his face red and puffy.

Ugh. Why had she gotten her hopes up?

After placing Colt into his bassinet, she stomped into the kitchen, his cries slashing at her heart. She sniffled while she prepared the formula, resisting the urge to bang and slam the cupboards. When the bottle was ready, Imani wiped the tears with the back of her hand and took a moment to gather herself before returning to feed her son. She didn't want him picking up on her distress.

As soon as she placed the bottle in his mouth, Colt began to gulp, swallowing hard. Poor thing was so hungry. It wasn't his fault his mother was…broken.

Ineffective.

Tears ran down her face. She consoled herself by repeating what Nash said, hoping to drown out the despondence. What was important was that Colt was getting what he needed. Hopefully, the more she repeated that, she would eventually be able to forgive herself.

Just as she finished burping the baby, there was a rap on the door.

Imani knew it wasn't Nash since he had a key, and it was only a little after 8:30 a.m. Tucking Colt close under her arm, she went to open the door. When she saw who stood there, she choked out, "How did you know?" Imani stepped aside to let her cousin inside. Nia had a gift in one hand and a take-out bag in the other. She placed the gift on the couch and the food on the coffee table. Imani's tummy rumbled. Whatever was inside smelled good. Imani scurried to put Colt down in his bassinet, then grabbed the baby monitor. Nia was right behind her.

Once her arms were free, Imani and Nia hugged and hugged, then hugged some more.

"You don't know how glad I am to see you, right now," Imani said once they had broken apart. Her cousin had brushed her hair in a bun and was dressed in a tapered pantsuit with patches of gold. "How was Paris?" she asked.

"Paris was dreamy and—" she patted her tummy "—I ate way too many beignets but I have no regrets."

Acutely aware of her disheveled state, Imani gathered

her hair at her nape and used the scrunchie on her wrist to secure it. She was still dressed in her jammies but at least she had brushed her teeth.

Nia's eyes narrowed. "Have you been crying?"

"I…" No point in denying it. Nia wasn't going to accept anything less than the truth. "A little bit." Imani plopped onto the couch and her cousin joined her. Clasping her hands in her lap, Imani said, "My milk is drying up and I can't provide for my child. I have to give Colt formula instead."

Nia shook her head. "Is something wrong with formula? Isn't that still providing?"

"I guess, but…" Imani lifted her shoulders. "A part of me knows it doesn't make sense but I feel like I failed Colt. I wanted to be good at motherhood. Check off all the must-dos from all the baby books I've read. Plus, I own a business that caters to babies but I can't do the same for my son. I feel guilty."

"How can you even begin to equate the two? You're approaching this wrong," Nia said, drawing closer. "You beat so many other statistics. Did you know that Black women are the least likely to survive delivery? You, my dear, are a walking miracle. Colt's being here is a miracle." She waved a hand. "The rest is just gravy. You'll figure it out."

Imani's mouth dropped. "I did know that. But, you read up on all that?"

"Yes, girl. You know I believe in research. But research has its limitations. There's also functioning. People beat statistics every day. Don't forget that."

"See, that's why we make such great business partners and cousins." The women shared another brief hug. "It is just gravy. I just wish I could get rid of this wedge of guilt in my heart."

"It will ease. You have to accept what you cannot control. If I know you, I know you tried. But for whatever reason, your body refused to cooperate and now you have to refocus on the benefits of using formula." Nia counted off her fingers, "Flexibility. You can get more help. Both you and baby can get more sleep."

"Wow. You really have been reading up on motherhood." She gave Nia a pensive look. "Anything I need to know?"

Nia held up both hands. "No—no children in the horizon for me. You know after Derek I don't do long-term. I speed date. Get what I need and get out. The books were just a great airplane read and I wanted to be prepared to help because I thought you were going to be a single parent and I was ready to be your sidekick." She changed topics. "But your life has been a whirlwind of late. Almost marrying one man and now getting back with your baby's father."

Imani felt her face warm. "I couldn't marry Simon knowing I wasn't in love with him especially when you and Mom and Grandma had bad vibes about his motivation."

"I'm so glad you didn't go through it because that would have been an absolute disaster. And being married to someone else would have been a major stumbling block in your and Nash's reunion." Nia's voice got dreamy. "You don't know how glad I am to hear the news. You both are my couple goals… Well, if I wanted a relationship."

"Nash and I aren't back together," Imani said stiffly.

Nia made a point of looking around the space. "Come again? Then why are you here? I know it's not because of financial reasons because the Porters make the Fortunes wealth seem like chump change. And you've always been

Miss Independent, so I can't think of any reason you'd be here if it wasn't a matter of the heart."

"It *is* a matter of the heart. Colt's heart. Colt deserves to know both his parents. Nash and I agreed that I would stay here for a few months while we get acclimated with parenthood. We haven't discussed anything beyond that point." Imani gestured toward the food bag.

"Help yourself. I bought us some breakfast burritos," Nia said with a wave. "You forget you're talking to someone who knows you. We slept in the same bed together at many sleepovers. I know all your secrets and you know mine. Your being here is a matter of your heart. Not just Colt's. I could understand if you stayed here a few days to recover, but if this was anybody but Nash, you would be long gone."

"But I—"

Her cousin held up a hand, determined to say her piece. "Now, don't get me wrong. This property is gorgeous and I'm hankering for a tour of the ranch, but if not for this man, you would be back at home. Nash Fortune has your heart and you're wishing and hoping for more, but you don't want to admit it."

Her words slammed Imani in the gut. "Am I that obvious?"

"Only to me. And probably Auntie and Grandma." Nia grabbed one of the sandwiches and took a big bite.

"The *more* I'm hoping for is all physical, though." She exhaled. "My body remembers oh-too well. I'm looking forward to resuming certain extracurricular activities with Nash once I get the all clear." That's all she could own up to.

Nia raised an eyebrow. "I'm calling your bluff. It's not just your body. Keep telling yourself that, though, but this *ayaba* ain't buying it." She peered into the baby monitor. "Hey! The little guy is awake. Can I go get him?"

"Sure."

Nia was gone and back with him in mere seconds. "It's beautiful out. Do you feel like going somewhere?"

Imani shrunk into the chair. She had to go out tomorrow with the baby and that would be traumatic enough. She wanted to chill inside today. That's one less day she would have to worry about Colt's lack of a great immune system. "How about we try out the swing instead?" Imani took Colt from his bassinet and buckled him into the swing. Then she put it on the lowest setting. Soft music played.

"Now, let's have you open your gift," Nia said.

Nia picked up the small rectangular package and handed it to her. It was a onesie that said, My Favorite Cousin Gave Me This, which made Imani smile, especially since Nia also had a matching shirt for her. She showered and then dressed in the shirt and a pair of jeans while Nia changed Colt. Watching her adept cousin struggle to get the article of clothing over his head was worth recording, much to Nia's chagrin. But once they were both ready, Nia had a mini photo session with all three of them. Imani had been delighted to see Nia's shirt under her jacket read, Their Favorite Cousin.

She sent Nash a couple of the photos when they were finished. Nia was now settled into the couch and was watching reality TV.

What a cute way to start my day, he texted. I'm on my way over in a few.

Her heart jumped. Avoiding her cousin's keen eye, she texted back: Nia wants a tour of the ranch.

That can be arranged. I know the owners, LOL. XOXO.

Whoa. She hoped Nash didn't think she planned on going. Just her cousin. And she told him as much.

You sure? It could be fun for Colt.

Yep.

He sent the thumbs-up emoji, followed with: I'll ask Jade. Grateful that Nash hadn't insisted she go on the tour, she addressed Nia to let her cousin know about it.

"Oh, that's exciting!" Nia said, clapping her hands.

"His sister Jade will probably be the one taking you around the property," Imani replied. Before Nia could ask why she wasn't going, Imani brought up the perfect distraction. "You can catch me up on what's going on with the additions at Lullababies while we wait for Nash."

Her cousin's eyes flashed. "Did you get my emails?" she squealed. "I sent you over three potential designs."

"I glanced at them but I've been helping Nash with a project so I didn't study them too much." She hid a smile. Nia loved talking shop.

"Me and the designer butt heads a bit but I think you'll be happy with the plans. I've got them in my car. Be right back." Nia rushed outside to get her laptop and the print-outs.

Colt seemed to be enjoying the swing, so she could pay attention to what her cousin wanted to share. She cleared the coffee table so Nia would have room for the blueprints. For the next twenty minutes, Nia went through the designs. Imani selected the second one that was spacious and had light decor and a warm color scheme.

"How did I know you would choose this?" Her cousin pumped her fists. "I've already ordered the supplies. By the time you're ready to come back to work, I think the expansion should be ready. I'll send you our publicity plans."

"I'm sure you can handle that without me." Imani rested a hand on Nia's arm. "I wanted to talk to you about something, actually."

Nia's enthusiasm waned. "What's going on?"

"I wanted to make you company head. I don't know yet if I want to come back to work full-time anytime soon."

"Is this about Nash? Don't think I didn't catch it when you said you were helping him with a project." Nia eyed her with suspicion. "You're getting all wrapped up in him again and I don't mind for the most part, unless it is interfering with our bottom line. And, to be clear, this feels like the bottom line."

"No, this is about me. How I'm feeling. I was actually thinking about selling you my shares to Lullababies." Nia gasped at her confession. "But Mom and Nash talked me out of it."

Nia's shoulders sagged. "Good, I'm glad because this is *both* of our dreams and I need you with me." She released a breath. "Then what is this about?"

"Since giving birth to Colt, my anxiety has been off-the-charts. I've never been so scared of everything in all my life. I've also never been more certain that I want to be there for every milestone of his development."

"So bring him to work. We own a baby business," Nia said. "If we can't accommodate real-life infants then we need to be doing something else."

"I just need…time." Her voice broke. "And I need you to be okay with my decision."

Nia hugged her close. "Alright, *ayaba*. Take all the time you need. I'm sorry if I overloaded you with all this shop talk."

"You didn't. It invigorated me," Imani said. "I just can't be involved one hundred percent in the day-to-day like before."

"Understood. Just promise me you'll talk to a professional if you get too overwhelmed."

Imani nodded. "I will."

Chapter Fourteen

It was just after 10:00 a.m. the morning of the fourteenth when Nash drove past Longhorn Feed, a quiver of excitement in his stomach. It had been a two-hour production getting themselves and Colt ready, along with all the just-in-case paraphernalia packed in his trunk, but they were out of the house and heading to the Daily Grind.

Imani kept peering behind her to check on Colt. Nash bit the inside of his cheek to keep from telling her that their son was alright. The only other place she felt comfortable going to with him was the doctor's office. Nash then distracted her by pointing out the orange and browns of the leaves and the different kinds of trees, and they discussed a possible venture to the pumpkin farm.

He pulled into the only empty space in the lot before opening the passenger door for Imani. Tilting his head up toward the sun and spreading his arms, Nash inhaled, his lungs expanding. "What a beautiful fall day for an outing with a beautiful woman. This is my favorite time of year."

"Thank you. It's mine, too, actually." Imani had dressed in a long-sleeved purple dress and paired it with boots the same color. She gave a jerky nod, shuffling from one foot to the other. If he didn't move now, she might change her mind.

Nash opened the rear door to lift the carrier, smiling

at his son, who looked at him with curious eyes. Imani had provided both Colt and Nash with matching checkered shirts that they had paired with dark blue jeans. "Hey, there, little fella." He had a preview of them spending Thanksgiving with his family and Christmas with hers, the three of them sporting coordinated outfits and found he liked that visual.

Imani grabbed the baby bag and stalled. "I don't know about this..."

"Imani, Colt has been around my entire family and yours. He'll be alright."

"But that's different. That's family. I don't know how I feel about Colt being exposed to a bunch of strangers. Not to mention how some people feel it's okay to be all up in a baby's face with their germs and hot breath." She gritted her teeth. "And they had better not use their dirty hands to squeeze his cheeks."

Oh, boy. Nash shifted the carrier to his other hand. "No one's going to do anything because we're here. And how are people we don't know going to get close to him unless we allow it?"

She snorted and visibly relaxed. "I know I sound ridiculous but I was reading up what to avoid when you take your newborn out in public places and you can't believe some of the stuff that goes on."

Oh, he could believe it. "Please stay off Google," Nash warned. "Yes, we need to be careful, but Colt needs to build up his immune system."

"I'd feel better if we came after he was past the two-month mark and had more of his immunization shots."

Nash opened the rear door and placed the carrier on the seat. Then he cupped Imani's cheeks. "Sweetheart, prepare yourself. He's going to eat paper, bugs and dirt. He's going to drink his bathwater, eat the pet's food, if we, er, either of us get one, and he's going to share his friend's lunches at school. And you know what? He will be just fine."

She wrinkled her nose. "How do you know all this?"

"Because I did it. My brothers and sisters did it, too, and we turned out just fine."

"Did you?"

He chuckled. "What I'm trying to say is that we can't keep Colt in a bubble. He's going to fall and scrape his knee. He might even break his front tooth and need to have it capped at ten years old. But that is a long way off and whatever happens, we will deal with it, and we will survive. Now, can we go inside and enjoy our lattes?"

She gave a jerky nod before grabbing his arm. "Wait. Did all that happen to you?"

"No comment." Nash picked up the carrier and closed the rear passenger door. Colt appeared to be falling asleep. His little head was tucked all the way in his chest. Then they headed inside the coffee shop. He loved the bustle around him. Right now, there were a few patrons bunched in the corner, waiting on their orders.

He waved at the workers and trailed after Imani, who had chosen a table the farthest away from the door. He placed Colt's carrier on the end of the table near the wall, and Imani sat facing him. Once they were settled, Nash joined the queue to place their orders—the caramel macchiato for her and an Americano for himself. He added a couple of scones and an everything bagel with cream cheese that they could split, then stifled a yawn. They had stayed up for a good two hours the night before sorting through more video recordings, distracting themselves by cracking jokes. He only had a few more videos to go through but he was sure he'd find the perpetrator. The culprit had been smart, avoiding the cameras, but Nash was counting on that person getting cocky and messing up.

And the good news was that Colt had slept for five hours. Five amazingly long, perfect hours. Nash had made sure to give their son more formula that morning and Imani hadn't had any objections.

Small steps with glorious, giant differences.

Their orders came up and he made his way back to the table, scooting his chair next to her. He loved the feel of her legs and arms brushing against his. It was sweet, electric... and *torture*. While they enjoyed their meal, they talked about their upcoming appointments the next day.

"My meeting with my family starts at nine, but we should be finished by ten thirty at the latest."

Imani took a sip of her latte, licking her lips. "You're right. This is delicious."

Nash put down his Americano and leaned over to give those luscious lips a taste. "You're so right. It is."

Her cheeks reddened but she strove for normalcy, her voice breathy. "I have a checkup with my ob-gyn and then Nia and I will have lunch and then our spa appointment at one o'clock."

"Yes, the owners have you down for massages, manicures and pedicures."

"Are you sure you'll be okay with Colt on your own?"

"Yep." He drummed his fingers on the tabletop. *There she goes tugging on those lips again.* He had to get another taste. But the perfume she wore distracted him, so he nuzzled her ear before getting another sample. Ooh, it was just as good as before.

"Nash, we're attracting attention," she whispered, running a finger down his cheek, her chest heaving.

He turned his head to see an older gentleman frowning

at them. The man sat near the entrance, holding the town paper in his hand, and he wasn't even trying to pretend not to stare. Nash didn't know if the older gentleman had a problem with them being an interracial couple or with their making out in public.

"Let's give him something to look at then." Nash had never had a problem with PDA, especially when it came to Imani. He wrapped an arm about her waist and kissed her like he hadn't had a drink in days. Oh, how he had missed this.

Forgetting about their audience, Nash explored her mouth thoroughly and she responded in kind with a low, throaty groan. It was only because Colt made a sound that they pulled apart. He was pleased to see they were now the only ones in the shop, the only other sounds the chatter of the workers and the grinding of the espresso machine. He placed a hand on Imani's thigh and gave it a squeeze. "I hope all goes well at the gynecologist's tomorrow." He waggled his eyebrows.

She slapped his hand and giggled. "It's only been two weeks and it should be a quick appointment. It'll be at least four more weeks before we can make love. Well, if we were, um, interested in that. Now, let's finish these delicious coffees before Colt gets up."

"How about we go for a stroll on the ranch when we're done here?" Nash suggested. "We can take a walk around the lake?"

"I'd like that," she said, lowering her lashes.

Nash couldn't hide his enthusiasm that they would be using one of Colt's two strollers for the first time later that day. Sabrina had chosen a designer stroller and car seat that was "all the rage" now because it was super-secure, lightweight and even had a privacy drape. Nash liked that it had foam and side-impact protection. Dahlia had urged him to get a jogging stroller as well since she knew Imani was a runner. Nash had placed that stroller in Imani's Jeep.

There was a light breeze that made the seventy-five-degree weather feel even more glorious. Before they left for their walk, Nash rushed into his house to get his hat and sunglasses. It was in the mid-70s and with these mild temperatures, it was hard to believe that Thanksgiving was so close. While he was at it, he decided to retrieve his mail. It had been a couple of days since he checked it. Among the usual junk mail, there was another envelope sealed with an emblem, just like the wedding invitation he had received.

Curious, he slid his finger under the seal to open it. His eyebrows rose. There were instructions enclosed:

Please choose a quote or passage from a book or movie or a loved one that captures how you feel about love and family. Maybe you'll even give a toast with it at the wedding...

After placing the card back into the envelope, Nash dropped it next to the invite. This mystery bride and groom seemed confident that he would attend, and now, it appeared as if he they were asking him to give a toast. He had to admit he was intrigued and he was already mulling over the request... Just in case. As he walked back to the guesthouse, Nash recalled something his mother always recited to him and his siblings before bed: *Good day, bad day, you are loved and love is everything.* With a demanding father like Casper, Nash had clung to those words like they were a lifeline. He wasn't too sure about love being everything, though.

Like he knew he loved Colt, but his devotion toward

his son wasn't enough. He had to be a good father, a good provider, a good caretaker. And in that, Nash knew he was sorely lacking. Seeing Imani waiting for him, Nash gave her a wave and jogged to her side.

"Ready to go?" she asked.

He took the handlebars and slapped on his ball cap and sunglasses. "Let's do this." They trekked down to the lake, stopping by the edge of the water, taking in the serenity. He slipped an arm around Imani's shoulder, bringing her close to him. She snuggled her head on his chest. Nash peered over her shoulder to see Colt was still asleep. "He sure does sleep a lot."

"I know, but he won't be like that for long. Soon, we'll be running after him and wishing for these days." Imani chuckled. That comment gave the impression that she had permanent intentions of sticking around, which made Nash hopeful.

"I can't wait until Colt is old enough for me to take him fishing."

His cell buzzed. It was Ridge. He sounded flustered when Nash answered. "We have a problem. I've got Arlo here with me."

He put the phone on Speaker and they turned back toward the guesthouse. "What's going on?"

Arlo jumped in. "Someone messed with the cattle feed. We found ground up metal shavings in the silage chopper. One of the farmhands heard noises in the machinery and stopped to investigate. That's when he found the ground-up pieces."

Imani's eyes went wide. They sped back to his place.

Nash expelled a breath, his strides long. "Wow. I can't believe someone is intentionally trying to destroy our cattle." His body chilled at that realization. Imani pushed the stroller even faster then.

"I know. This could have caused serious internal damage to the cows if they had ingested it," Ridge said.

"Or, it could have killed them," Arlo muttered. "We lost a couple hundred acres of silage."

He whistled. "I... Wow. I can't even wrap my mind around this. How did they do it?"

"They tied metal around the corn stalks."

"But how could we have missed this?" Nash asked.

"I think they did it over time. This was obviously planned. The deputies are on their way back. Turns out this kind of mischief happened a few months ago on another ranch a few hours away. That was never solved, either, so they really want to get their hands on the recordings."

He dashed into the guesthouse, welcoming the blast of air. "I don't have much video footage left to go. I'll finish going through them since I don't think the deputies will be back until late. In the meantime, keep me posted." Nash ended the call.

Imani smoothed her dress with her hands. "I'll order lunch and we can finish going through the videos together." Without waiting for an answer, she said, "Let me go get my laptop."

We.

Together.

Those words were a balm to his heart, flaring hope and weaving an even stronger bond than he and Imani had shared before, a sense of belonging. Of family.

And he was there for it. All of it.

Chapter Fifteen

"It's about time you called to check out your nephew," she said. Sitting against the headboard, Imani smiled at the familiar face on her screen. "Even Dad beat you to it." Phillip had called for a few minutes to check on her, but she had been too exhausted to talk much.

Her eyes felt gritty from lack of sleep but she was too caffeinated and excited to fall asleep just yet. It was now 2:00 a.m. and Nash had laid down on the couch, tuckered out but relieved. They had found the perpetrator and he would be sharing that news with his family at their business meeting later that morning.

But since it was only 11:00 a.m. in Dubai, Imani had texted Jonathan a picture of Colt dressed in a two-piece sweater set that had a little fluffy lamb on the chest. With their living in different time zones, they communicated most of the time through text messages. But every now and again, Imani craved to hear her brother's voice.

"I know, but between you and Mom, I have tons of pictures to keep me up to speed." His eyes sparkled. She took in the familiar brown eyes, chiseled jaw and a perfect smile created by the top dentist in Texas. No one could tell he had been born with oversize front teeth, something Imani never made him forget. Like a good sister, she had called him Chipmunk during his middle-school years.

"You actually caught me at a good time. I'm in between meetings." He glanced at his watch. "I've got about ten minutes before I have to go."

"My heart is happy to see your beautiful face," she said, angling her iPad so Jonathan could get a good view of Colt.

"Likewise. Oh, look at the baby. He's all bundled up," Jonathan said, in a higher pitch than his normal bass voice. She had swaddled him and rested him on a baby blanket on the other side of the king-size bed. Her son was awake, and looking her way. She rubbed his tummy. Colt gave a sweet reflexive grin, a tiny dimple in his right cheek on display. She couldn't wait until he started smiling for real in a few weeks.

Jonathan addressed her. "So what's this I hear about you selling Lullababies? Are you finally about to grant Grandpa his wish and take over the family business stateside? It would be good to partner with you. *Finally.* Like we planned."

Hearing his desire for them to join forces made her gut twist with nostalgia. Since they were eighteen months apart, they had been reared like twins, making them closer as siblings. But she knew her brother would support her decision.

"Um…one of the reasons why I was thinking about selling my portion of the business to Nia was because we're branching out to offer exclusive baby-shower experiences, which means more hours and more work. But there's no way I would put down a molehill and pick up a gargantuan mountain that's Porter Oil."

"Whoa. I always figured you would do both—keep your company and lead Porter Oil in the US. You can scout for the right staff to assist you as needed with both. Grandpa has been preparing you to lead Porter Oil from the moment you could walk and talk." Hmm… Grandpa must not have approached Jonathan yet about taking over in her stead. Imani decided not to mention it. She would leave that for her grandfather to do when he was ready.

"That was my intention…before Colt."

"Wow, sis. Becoming a parent seems like a huge paradigm shift."

"Yes, but it's one I find myself eager to do. I welcome the changes. I have a child to raise, and I don't want to be an absentee parent."

"Yeah… I wouldn't want to be that kind of parent, either."

"Both Nash and I had that in common—though our dad wasn't anything like his—but regardless, we want to be involved in Colt's life. I need to be there for each precious moment."

"Whew. Parenting sounds like it requires major sacrifices, which is why I don't plan on having any children," he scoffed.

Her eyebrows rose. "Not at all?"

"Nope."

"Be careful, bro. Life has a way of making you eat your words," she joked, thinking of how committed she had been to her business. A commitment now surpassed by the infant mere inches away from her.

"Not the life I have planned," he countered. Jonathan sounded so sure, Imani had to remind him of her experience.

"Neither Nash nor I knew when we broke up that we would be welcoming a baby six months later."

His brow furrowed and he cocked his head. "So what's

up with all the me-and-Nash comments? Did I miss the memo? Are you two back together?"

"Well, I don't know exactly... I'd say we're co-parenting."

He arched an eyebrow. "And cohabitating?"

"I'm staying in the guesthouse," she said, her voice firm. "Nash stays here on the couch at times to help me with Colt." How could she define their current relationship status when she needed clarity herself? Yes, they had shared tender moments, touches and steamy kisses, but that was all physical. Imani knew she wouldn't take their attraction to mean more than that. She wouldn't make any assumptions. The last time she had, it had led to her and Nash's breakup.

"Ha! Okay, just be careful. I don't want this dude hurting you again," he said, his voice holding an edge.

"Stand down. Might I remind you that I'm the older sibling? I've got this. I don't interfere in your personal life, so you need to take your foot out of mine."

He exhaled and ran a hand across his beard. "Okay, sis. I'll leave it alone. *For now.* I know that Nash is good people but I'll never forget that he wasn't there throughout your entire pregnancy."

"Jonathan, for the umpteenth time, he didn't know I was expecting," she groaned.

"But he would have, if he hadn't run you off."

"Ugh." She ran a hand through her curls and drew in deep breaths. "It's pointless arguing with you." She appreciated her brother being her champion but she was more than capable of handling her own messy affairs.

"I agree," he teased. "Well, I've got to go but don't allow that man back in your bed until you are sure of his intentions." He disconnected before she could respond. Imani released a long plume of air. Typical Jonathan. Goodness, that man liked to have the last word.

Right as she ended the call, Imani noticed Nash loung-
ing against the doorjamb. He had changed into a pair of
pajamas that hung off his waist, but because he was shirt-
less, those abs were in full view. She swallowed. Was it
her or was he looking extra ripped? Her insides ached to
get a touch. Dragging her eyes upward, she noticed he had
a self-satisfied smirk on his face. The man knew he was
beyond fine.

He strutted into the room and came over to kiss her on
the cheek. Tease. "I heard voices and came to investigate."
His breath smelled minty and fresh, making Imani all too
aware of the tuna-fish sandwich she had had earlier.

"I was talking to my brother," she said. "It's late morning there." She stood, pointing to the baby, and placed a
finger over her lips.

"He's up?" Nash whispered, his eyes filled with delight.
This man had better not start playing with the baby. Imani
needed Colt to get used to sleeping at night.

With a nod, she gestured for Nash to keep an eye on
their son and went to brush her teeth and take care of her
nightly rituals. When she returned, he was alternating between playing with the baby's feet and rubbing his nose
in Colt's tummy. The baby was bright-eyed, his little fists
bunched, and watching his daddy. She wondered what
Colt was thinking. Did newborns even have thoughts? She
needed to look that up.

"Quit messing with him," she chided gently. "Unless
you want to pull another all-nighter?"

Nash stopped immediately. "Does he need a diaper
change?"

Imani hid a smile. He had become quite the expert. She
could tell he was proud of that. "No, I just changed him and

fed him. He should be good. The only thing left for him to do is get back to sleep."

Colt emitted a sigh before yawning. "Aww, somebody's ready for a nap," Nash said, picking him up and cuddling him against his chest. "Daddy will rock you to sleep." He began to hum some lullaby off-key, then whispered, "I love you." Imani's chest expanded at the sight. She reached for her iPad and snapped a picture. The scene was so sweet and authentic that her eyes misted.

That's something Colt would miss out on once they were back home in Cactus Grove. His father's touch. Imani pulled up her phone and typed *How important is a father's touch?* in the internet search bar. She read the first thing that popped up and it basically said that a father's touch was equally important as a mother's. Physical contact is a crucial part of a child's development between parents and their child.

Huh. Wasn't that something? As an adult, she craved Nash's touch, but she was ready to put on her proverbial big-girl boxers when the time came and let that go. But Colt was just a baby. He couldn't advocate or express for himself how the absence of his father affected him.

However, she could.

And so could Nash.

They both knew what that felt like and those feelings didn't disappear. They intensified. They dictated their actions even as grown-ups. Now, she had a father who was devoted to her when he was around, so there was that. But look at Nash. He had been petrified, was still petrified, with embracing fatherhood because of the kind of father he had had. Because he had lacked a father's touch.

She wiped away the impending tears. She couldn't have Colt feeling the same lack of affection. Not when she had the means to do otherwise. Maybe she could look at a place in town or something… She would figure it out. A light snore made her refocus on Nash and Colt.

They were both asleep. Another picture worth taking. But if she settled nearby, it wouldn't be the last.

Chapter Sixteen

From where he stood on the veranda at the LC Club, which overlooked Lake Chatelaine, Nash could hear the water trickling and the birds chirping on this sunny mid-November morning, though it was a bit muggy for this time of year. But a beautiful day nevertheless for good news. Nash had arranged for a large spread of varied breakfast items, as well as fruit with an omelet stand.

He scanned each of the tables on the veranda where his family—his mom, Dahlia and Rawlston, Sabrina and Zane, Heath and Jade, Ridge and his mystery woman, Hope, as well as Arlo—had gathered for their strategic meeting. Everyone except Imani, whom he had advised to sleep in with Colt after their long night.

"Before we officially begin this meeting," Nash said, "I wanted you to know that after reviewing countless hours of footage, Imani and I found the perpetrator early this morning. I've handed over the footage and the police are arresting Roger Pitts as we speak."

Collective gasps could be heard around the veranda, followed by collective applause.

"We need a more rigorous application and screening process," Arlo called out. "We'll work on that.

"Agreed." Nash hated that it was someone he had employed who did this but the deputies assured him that Roger had conned many other ranch owners as well. The man's next step would have been to approach Nash to "investigate" and pin the deed on someone else while pocketing a good chunk of money.

"Way to go, bro," Ridge said, coming over to slap him on the back. He was holding six-month-old Evie in the crook of his arm. "Tell Imani 'thank you' for us."

"I will, but why don't you tell her yourself? How about you and Hope come over later so we can catch up. I'm sure she and Hope would hit it off."

"Alright. I'll let Hope know and get back with you." Ridge looked so comfortable holding the little girl and everyone in the family could see he was crazy about his houseguest and baby Evie.

Nash slapped his forehead. "Wait. Let's plan for another day instead. I forgot that I'm on baby duty later so Imani can go to lunch and a spa appointment with her cousin."

"Okay, talk it over with her and I'll wait to hear from you." Just then Evie grabbed Ridge's nose. Nash and Ridge cracked up trying to free it.

"That's some grip," Nash joked.

"Yeah, there's nothing stronger or faster. You'll see."

Nash's stomach clenched. *Would he?* Imani had promised him four months. And, of that time, fourteen days had whipped by already.

"Hey, Nash, quit your lollygagging and get on with the rest of the meeting," Jade called out. "Some of us have places to go and people to see." She was the only of his sisters to have dark hair and hazel eyes.

"You just saying that because you want to get back to your petting zoo and the kids." He smirked. "You can hang with us bigger humans for a little bit."

She tossed a Danish toward him. Nash ducked and it landed somewhere over the fence. From his peripheral view, he saw one of the servers scamper to pick it up and gave them a wave. He would leave an even more generous tip.

"Quit it, you two," Wendy called out from the other end. "But I agree with Jade, let's get this meeting going. It's starting to get muggy out here. And we didn't even talk about Thanksgiving yet."

"It will be at your house," Sabrina announced. "We'll show up in time to eat. Planning over."

Dahlia snickered right along with the rest of the fam. Wendy rolled her eyes, but Nash knew his mother was secretly pleased. She enjoyed preparing and overseeing the family feast each year.

"I'll delegate who's bringing what in the group chat," Wendy said.

"Snap, snap," Jade said. Heath placed an index finger over her lips. Just like that, they only had eyes for each other. He reached in to give her a kiss.

"Ugh. Get a room," Arlo called out. He was the only person unattached at the moment—well, besides Mom—and he apparently intended to remain that way.

At his comment, the other couples began to smooch just to tease Arlo. Nash loved seeing his sisters really happy and in healthy relationships.

"I don't get why whenever you all get together, you're back to acting like children again," Wendy chided, fanning her face.

Of course, that made Nash think of Imani. He missed her. And he hadn't kissed her that morning. He planned to rectify that as soon as he got home. Clearing his throat, Nash asked everyone to pull up the plans he had emailed the night before on their devices.

"Our first order of business now that our ranch is no longer under attack is to discuss our plans for supplying local business and restaurants with our Black Angus cows. Since we aren't the only ranch in the area, I say we target five-star restaurants."

"Good idea. We can start with this very club," Ridge said.

"Yes, I say we prepare a proposal to pitch them in five months or so. We should have doubled our Angus cows by then. How does that sound?" Arlo asked.

"That will work." He tilted his head toward Jade. "How are your educational programs with the petting zoo going?"

"They are going well," his twin said, giving him a thumbs-up. "I'll email you an update."

"Fair enough." Nash swiped his iPad to his next bullet point. "I was also thinking that one of the things we could do is breed racehorses. We certainly have enough land space for this. What do you think?" All heads turned to Dahlia since she used to be a Texas junior champion barrel racer as a teen. She'd also worked as a groom at the racetracks.

"While I think racehorses would be a good investment, breeding quarter horses is a much better choice, since they are versatile and trainable."

"That a great suggestion, Dahlia." Nash jotted some notes on his plan.

"Quarter horses?" Wendy asked.

"Yes, they are a mix of Arabian and mustang," Dahlia further explained. "You can't go wrong with that investment. I'll scout around and purchase our first set of horses."

"And I'll review what we have so far and prepare our budget and potential profit-and-loss," Sabrina added, ever the numbers woman. Of all the siblings, she'd inherited her father's money skills the most. And, as such, she took her role as ranch accountant very seriously. When they first moved, Nash had squabbled with her over the brand of paper clips to purchase at the GreatStore. *Paper clips.*

Sabrina then shared their projected earnings and expenses for the remainder of the year and they recorded potential future ventures. Nash decided to plug in a couple dates on their calendars for them to meet again.

Everyone agreed, although he could see their general vibe was "we have more money than we could ever spend in this lifetime or the next." But still, as the ranch foreman, he felt these meetings were important in establishing good working practices.

With the meeting adjourned, Nash hugged all the members of his family, which took some time. But he made it back to the guesthouse in time to help with Colt, so Imani could get dressed for her doctor's appointment and spa date with Nia. Nash used that time to fill her in on the meeting and also on Ridge's intention to visit. Imani told him to confirm for the following day. She told him she had washed the baby bottles for when Colt awakened.

Before she left, she asked once again if he was okay being on his own with Colt.

"I'll be alright."

"Okay, well, Wendy said to call or text if you need anything."

Ignoring his pounding heart, Nash repeated, "I'll be alright."

Imani lifted her index finger. "One more thing…" She fretted with her bottom lip. "I think I want to stay here in Chatelaine Hills indefinitely."

Wow. His heart sang. "I would love that."

"Yeah, I'm going to go house hunting in the upcoming weeks."

His stomach dropped. "Oh, I thought…" Nash ran his

hands through his hair. "I mean, you could stay here..."
Things between them were going well and he hoped in time
Imani would love him again. That they could be a family unit.

She bit on her bottom lip "I don't know if that's a good
idea, especially since we're not *together* together."

Nash stood and got into her space. "I'm not kissing
anybody else." He snatched her close to him, appreciating
her sharp intake of breath. Rocking his hips into hers, he
slipped his hand under her shirt and mumbled in her ear.
"I'm not trying to get close with anyone else."

"Me, either. We can be co-parents with benefits... No
lasting commitments. No expectations," she breathed out,
her hands going around his neck.

"If that's what you want." That was so not what he desired but he wasn't about to reject such an enticing offer.
Knowing she was right next door had kept him awake for
more hours than he could ever admit. The scent of jasmine
teasing his nostrils, his hands found their way into those
lustrous curls, and he kissed her neck.

She moaned and tilted her head back, her hands gripping his shoulders and that desirable mouth open. Waiting.
Nash crushed his lips to hers, their tongues engaging in a
hot tango. They heard a honk.

Nia had arrived. They broke apart, his mouth already
hungering for more. Imani wobbled her way to the door.
His chest puffed at her disorientation.

"Hurry back," he teased.

Once she was gone, Nate grew serious. He rubbed his
chin. Oh, he would go along with this scheme of hers. For
now. But he intended to turn the heat way up. For if things
went according to *his* plan, at the end of the four months,
Imani would be a permanent fixture in his bed...and in
his life.

Chapter Seventeen

"How was the tour yesterday?" Imani asked as soon as she strapped in her seat belt in Nia's Porsche. She struggled to sound normal and not like someone who had been kissed thoroughly mere minutes ago.

"Why are you all flushed?" Nia asked. "Were you and Nash sucking face in there?"

"Gosh, nothing gets by you. If you had any decency, you would pretend not to see."

"And miss out of the fun of seeing your cheeks red with embarrassment? No way." Her cousin put the car in gear. On the way to her doctor's appointment, Nia filled her in on the tour. "The grounds are spectacular and Jade is so passionate about her petting zoo. I had a lot of fun feeding the animals. But the horses were my favorite. Man, it's been a minute since I've gotten on the saddle, but I might have to before I leave for Cactus Grove tomorrow morning." She released a breath. "I was still tired and jet-lagged last night, but Jade said I could come back this evening. Mom is preparing a welcome-home luncheon for me even though I told her I was only gone for a couple of weeks, so I've got to hit the road by nine. You want to come with?"

"I'll pass this time," Imani said, missing Colt already. "I don't want to leave Nash too long with the baby. This is his first time watching him on his own and my first time leaving Colt and I'm a bit nervous." She glanced at her watch. They had only been gone for five minutes. Good grief, she didn't know if was going to make it. "Maybe I should cancel the spa appointment. I feel like I'm abandoning my son." She slid a glance Nia's way. "Do you mind?"

Nia pursed her lips. "I mind for *your* sake. You need this more than you know. I understand your concern and I respect it, Imani, but you're using words like *abandoned* when Colt is with his father." She patted the steering wheel. "Nash will call for help if he needs it."

"I—I supposed you're right." She turned to look out the window, admiring the passing scenery. "By the way, I'm going to connect with a Realtor to look for something more permanent here in Chatelaine Hills."

Nia stomped on the brakes, then pulled over near the entrance of the ranch. "Girl, I can't keep up with you! You're giving me a mental whiplash. You want to *move* here? Won't that make things harder for you emotionally when Nash decides he's done with fatherhood?"

Imani winced. "First, Nash intends to be a full-time father. Second, I want Colt to have the benefits of both parents if that's possible. I was doing some research online and—"

Nia slumped. "Oh, spare me the research right now. I like living in the penthouse next door to you." She continued, "I recognize that I'm being extremely selfish right now when you're only doing what's best for you and Colt. And you don't need me throwing a tantrum. You need me in your corner rooting for you." She sighed. Imani opened her mouth but Nia was still caught up in her meltdown. Her cousin clasped her hands and looked up. "I just hope this man treats you right." Nia reached over and patted Imani's hand then exhaled. "Pretty soon, you'll both declare your undying love for each other and all will be well in your world again. Okay, good talk. Good talk." She put the Porsche in Drive and they continued on their way.

After a routine visit with the gynecologist, the women made their way over to the spa. On their way, Imani texted Nash to check on Colt. She had pulled up the app but Colt wasn't in his crib.

How is he?

He's fine. Nash sent a photo of Colt in his arms.

Her heart melted. I miss him. I'm having an extreme case of separation anxiety.

That's normal. Take a deep breath. Have fun.

I'll try.

Don't try. Do.

"Girl, put your phone away," Nia advised. "If it makes you feel better, Colt doesn't even remember you to miss you. He's a newborn. He won't have object permanence until about four months or so. How's that for a fun fact?"

"No, it doesn't make me feel better and there's nothing fun about that tidbit you just shared." She dropped her phone in her purse and clutched it close. "To use your words, spare me the research right now."

Nia chuckled. "Touché. Okay, I'll use a different approach. If you're planning to get intimate with Nash soon, it's a good idea to get your lawn mowed, and your trees trimmed. You don't want the man lost in a forest, if you get my drift."

"Ugh." She covered her face. "Can we talk about something else…please?" The ob-gyn had reported that she was healing nicely and had even declared her good for intercourse at the four-week mark instead of six. Plus, her abdomen had shrunk and Imani was nearly back to her prebaby weight.

"You know I've got no filter when I'm hanging with you," Nia said, unapologetic. "All throughout my day, whether I'm at work or traveling, I've got to have my friendly face on. I've got to watch the way I act, the way I speak, or people might see me as the proverbial angry Black woman. It's refreshing to not have to worry about any of that with you. I can just be me."

"I get it."

"I know you do. Add all that to being a woman in business where you have your every move questioned. It's *exhausting*."

Imani knew Nia had been frustrated with the designer counteracting her ideas, but she hadn't seen how that impacted her. "Do you want me to fire the contractor?" she asked. "He gets paid to meet your asks, not to question your choices."

"No. I can handle him. I just don't want to operate on the offensive all the time." She turned into the spa entrance. "That's why I'm looking forward to this massage and being pampered. Plus, I have this cute design I want when we get our mani-pedis. I hope the technician has the skills to pull it off."

Imani vowed not to ruin Nia's good time. They gathered their purses and headed inside.

"I'm getting a burnt orange color, and beige since Thanksgiving is coming up," Imani said, inhaling the scents of vanilla and mint. Now that she was here, Imani found she was looking forward to some girl time.

"That sounds cute."

They placed their belongings in lockers and changed into the fluffiest robes she had ever worn. Then they headed to get their massages. Nia had chosen the stone massage while Imani had gone with aromatherapy. Midway through, her cousin started groaning and moaning so much that Imani knew she was blushing.

"Girl, will you quit with all that noise. You're getting a massage, not having sex."

"Ooh, this feels way better," Nia said, while the masseuse kneaded her back muscles. "Not that I haven't gotten sex. I've had plenty for your information. While I was in France, I met this Swedish dude—"

Imani's head popped up. "Wait, *Swedish*? I thought you were only all about the brothers." Her masseuse gently pressed her shoulders, a cue for her to lie back down.

"Well, as you said, don't knock it 'til you try it." Nia giggled. "And tried it I did. I must have sampled that about four or five times and if I had to rate it, I'd give it five stars."

"You are a hot mess." Imani chuckled. "I'm glad you're getting back out there after Derek, even if you're—" she put up air quotes "—just sampling." Derek had been Nia's first love and he had hurt her cousin so bad that Imani wasn't sure that Nia would ever fully recover.

"Derek who?" Nia scoffed. "It's all about Magnus now."

Imani's mouth dropped. "Magnus? Really? That's his name?"

"Girl, blame his mama. I didn't do that."

"I forgot how much fun you are. I'm glad I did this."

The women shared a laugh. While they had their mani-pedis, they each had smoothies and even added a facial and waxing to their spa plan. When they walked out of the spa salon, Imani lifted her hands. "That was an amazing experience. I feel like a whole new woman."

"Great because I booked you several appointments for the next four months when I was leaving my tip."

The cousins engaged in small talk all the way back to the guesthouse. She noticed that Nash's Range Rover was missing. She pushed the door open to the guesthouse and was greeted with quiet. Where was he? Nia rushed into the bedrooms, calling out for Nash.

Imani's heart galloped like a racehorse. She dug into her purse and pulled out her phone but there was no message from him. She placed a hand over her mouth. "What if something happened to my baby?" Her knees buckled and her chest tightened. "Please. No. Not that. My baby. My baby." Her shoulders shook and her body trembled.

Nia rushed over to take her hand. "Nash would have called or texted if anything was wrong." Then she made her take long breaths. "He's okay. Colt is okay," she soothed.

At that moment, she heard a car door slam. Nia helped her stand. The lock turned and Nash entered, holding Colt in his carrier. "Oh, good. You're back. How was your visit?" He gave them a wary glance.

"We had…a great time," Nia said, trailing off, giving Imani's arm a quick squeeze.

Imani blinked rapidly. How dare he sound so calm when he had disappeared without telling her his whereabouts! Anger pulsed through her veins. "Where were you?" she demanded.

Nash's eyes widened. "Twenty minutes after you left, I started feeling nervous so I took Colt to my mother's house." Wow. He hadn't lasted past twenty minutes on his own. "On my drive back, Colt became fussy and I figured a longer ride would help him fall asleep and it worked."

"That was a great idea," Nia said, looking between them. It was obvious her cousin was trying to signal at her to remain calm, but forget that. She was furious and he was going to know it.

Imani bunched her fists. "So you left the house with my child without leaving a note? Or texting me?"

"*Your* child?" he asked, his voice like steel.

"Yes. My son."

Nash placed Colt on the couch. She could see the fury emanating off him in waves, but she wasn't about to apologize. Nia picked up Colt and whispered to Nash, "She's just worried," then scampered into the nursery with the baby.

Nash faced her, eyes flashing. "Don't you ever say something like that to me again. My name is on his birth certificate right next to yours. I would never put our son in harm's way." Imani opened her mouth to snap back, but he spoke first. "Think long and hard before you say something you'll regret. You're spiraling right now because you're in mama-bear mode, but I'm going to need you to bring it down. Way down."

They faced off. Her temper was at a whirlwind but her breathing normalized and rational thought returned.

Whoa. He was right.

But shoot, so was she. "I apologize. I went too far just now. I panicked when I didn't know where Colt was." Imani massaged her temples. "However, in the future, it would be extremely helpful if you communicated when you're leaving with Colt. It helps with my anxiety. I'm just afraid of something happening to him."

"That's fair. I'm sorry I didn't think to leave a note. That's a good idea. I promise to do that next time." Nash came over and pulled her into him. She molded her body into his. "I've never seen you lose your temper before, and I don't think I want to see that anytime soon."

Imani melted into him, welcoming his strength and then pulled out of his arms. Reluctantly. "I'm usually more even-keeled. Frankly, I'm surprised at my reaction." She dipped her head to her chest. "Now I feel silly for overreacting but I genuinely felt like something catastrophic had happened to Colt. It's hard to explain the sensation."

"Don't." Nash gathered her close once more, then kissed the top of her head before trailing kisses across her neck. "Hmm… You smell amazing…and your skin feels like butter." Imani smirked. It was obvious he was ready to forget the past few minutes, but she couldn't. Nash was being very understanding but this freak-out was a wake-up call. Imani needed balance in navigating the new feelings that came with motherhood. She was going to schedule an appointment with a therapist tomorrow morning. Feeling better already now that she'd made that decision, she lowered her hands to cup his firm butt.

"I guess that means you all have settled your dispute," Nia said wryly.

Nash and Imani sprang apart.

"Oh, snap, I forgot that you were here," Imani said. "Did you want to stay for dinner?"

"Naw. I'm not about to be a third wheel," Nia joked. "Actually, Jade texted that she was ready to meet up at the stables. We're going to get dinner after that." She walked over with her arms spread wide. "So let's say our goodbyes from tonight." She gave Nash a hug and he gave her a friendly salute before going into the nursery. Then Nia strutted over to Imani. The women embraced and rocked and hugged some more.

"Thanks for today," Imani said, rubbing her cousin's back. "I needed it."

"You are so welcome."

Imani's took her cousin's hand and whispered, "I'm going to make an appointment to talk to someone."

Her cousin rested her forehead against hers. "I'm so glad to hear that."

Would you know her cousin refused to leave, but stood there with her arms folded until Imani had scheduled her first session? Nia just warmed her heart.

Chapter Eighteen

It wasn't postpartum depression. At least he didn't think so.

Not that he was any kind of expert. Nash sat outside on his porch doing research while Imani and Colt went for a walk. Imani's rage the night before had stemmed from genuine fear and all he wanted to do was comfort her. Help her. Based on her symptoms, she appeared to be struggling with maternal separation anxiety.

Common for new mothers.

That was a relief to know. He massaged the back of his neck and exhaled. He just needed to be patient and encourage her to verbalize her feelings. Then he would do his best to put her at ease.

Feeling satisfied that he had a game plan, Nash texted Imani to let her know he was going by the ranch for a bit. They had purchased a new feeder and he wanted to see for himself that everything was working as it should.

She texted back: I ordered salmon, whipped potatoes and salad from the LC Club for dinner. Are your brother and Hope still coming by tonight?

Okay. Yes.

Can you pick up the order on your way back?

Happy to.

When he arrived at the ranch, he was pleased to see his mother hanging about. She had stopped by to post a catered Thanksgiving menu for the ranch hands and their families. They planned to set up tents, tables and chairs and decorate the day before. Then the set-up crew would break everything down the next day. This was something Wendy intended to do every year as a means of appreciation for their workers right along with giving them a bonus. That was in addition to the bonus the workers would receive during the Christmas holiday season.

"This is such a thoughtful idea, Mom," Nash said, taking the signs and taping them in the break room.

"Thank you, son. Luckily, I was able to find caterers willing to come out and set up on Thursday afternoon."

"I think the ranch hands will be gratified by your efforts." Nash rubbed his chin. "I wonder if we can get a little band out, make it a bigger celebration."

Wendy's eyes lit up. "I like the idea of having a band. I'll check on that. If I can't arrange it this year, then definitely next year."

"Well, I can contribute as well. Or, we can check with Sabrina to see if we can cover this using our petty funds?"

Wendy waved a hand. "I'll just take care of it since this is last-minute planning. We can consult with Sabrina to set it up that way next year."

"Did you need me to do anything for our own Thanksgiving meal?"

"I think between me and the girls, we're good. But if you want to bring some pies or something that would be great." Wendy cocked her head. "How's my grandbaby doing?"

Nash's chest puffed. "He's getting bigger every day."

"Yes, he'll be walking around before you know it." Her eyes had a faraway look in them, like she was reminiscing.

"I can't imagine what it must have been like running after six of us."

She smiled. "Oh, it was wild and crazy and fun all at the same time. The years go by in a flash." Then she pinned him with a gaze. "Treasure every moment. Because years down the road, that's all you've have—fond memories and photos."

"I hope my son will have fond memories of me," he said, then snorted. "I still have this lingering fear that I'm not doing a good enough job with him and for him."

"You're here and you're loving Colt. That's what matters."

Nash's heart squeezed. He had been so busy with Colt that he hadn't visited with his mother in a while. Wendy shook her head like she was shaking off the memories and planted a kiss on his cheek. "I've got to run, but tell Imani I'll be stopping by soon. Thanks for the pictures and videos that you've sent me. They have been such a delight." Then with a two-finger wave, she said, "We'll catch up soon."

Nash walked his mother out. Was it him or did she have an added dose of enthusiasm and energy these days? She seemed to have an extra bounce in her step. Maybe it was because she was a grandmother now. It appeared that the move out here to Chatelaine had been a good choice. His heart lifted. His mother had spent so many years unhappy that he was glad to see her excited about this Thanksgiving feast. There was nothing his mother enjoyed more than having all her children around her.

After checking on the feeder, Nash was pleased to see all was as it should be. He also took the time to visit with

Stanley, who had returned to the stables from his leave that morning.

"I'm right as rain," Stanley said, while giving Onyx a brush-down. "Truth be told, I could have come back to work the next day because I was worried about not getting a pay-check. But Miss Dahlia told me to take the full two weeks off to recuperate. With pay." He touched his chest. "I'm so glad to be working for such a caring family."

"We are happy to have you," Nash said, giving him a pat on the back. "How are Penelope and Valentina getting along?"

"You remembered their names?" Stanley eyes were wide as saucers. "They are both doing good. Penelope is about ready to crawl."

"Good to hear. Give them my regards."

"Yes, sir. I'll let them know you asked about them." Stanley cocked his head toward the stables. "Midnight and Leviathan could use a stretch. Those horses are such beauties. Miss Jade and her guest took them out yesterday."

He must be talking about Imani's cousin, Nia. Nash smiled. "Go ahead and take them out, but be careful. I'll be back for a longer visit soon. Don't stay too late." Hopefully, Imani would be down to go horseback riding with him. He looked at his watch. She would probably be done with her walk, and he wanted to be there when she returned.

As he was about to climb into his vehicle, a car pulled up and parked in the visitor parking. It looked to be a newer-model silver station wagon. Nash peeped at the Audi logo. A middle-aged couple exited the wagon and gave him a friendly wave. They were both dressed in blue jeans and tweed shirts although he had on a cowboy hat.

"I'm sorry but if you're here for the tour, our last one has already ended."

"We would love that. On the drive up, we were talking about how your property is beautiful and well-tended," the man said, splaying his hands. Nash surveyed the fall foliage, the deep oranges and yellows and browns, adding to the picturesque view.

"I saw your face on the billboard in town," the woman added. "That picture doesn't do you justice."

"Thank you, I guess."

"Do you get a lot of visitors?"

That was an odd question. Nash raised an eye brow. "It depends on the day. We have a vast property and a lot going on throughout the day."

The couple looked at each other before the man stepped forward. He shoved his vein-filled hands into his pockets. "I wonder if you know if a woman and a baby might have stopped here a few months ago. She has long auburn hair and blue eyes."

"Her baby looks just like her. Can't be more than about six months old or so," the woman said, wiping her brow. Her hand shook a little.

Their question seemed innocent enough, but their tone held an undercurrent of desperation that didn't sit well with him. "Sorry, I don't think I've seen anyone fitting that description. And even if that were the case, we get so many visitors, it would be hard for me to comment."

Both faces dropped. The older gentleman used the tip of his boot to scuff the packed earth, then asked, "You sure about that?"

A knot formed in his stomach, but Nash shrugged. "I don't recall."

The couple thanked him and drove off. Nash watched their departure until they were out of sight. He exhaled. The truth was, he *did* know someone who fit that description.

A mystery woman in a barn with a baby bearing a strong resemblance. He texted Ridge.

Have I got something to tell you!

After they had eaten and Imani opened the gift from Hope—a pair of infant rattle socks—the two couples settled in the living-room area. Hope and Imani had hit it off upon meeting, bonding over motherhood, with Hope sharing more of what to expect. He had overhead Imani whispering to the other woman about her inability to breastfeed. Nash hadn't heard Hope's response, but whatever she said boosted Imani's spirits. Evie and Colt were now asleep in the nursery, with Colt in the bassinet and Evie in the crib.

"So what's going on?" Ridge asked, seated next to Hope. Nash joined Imani on the love seat.

"An older couple stopped by the ranch earlier this evening." Nash jutted his chin toward Hope. "I think they were asking about you."

Hope stilled. "Me?" She glanced at Ridge, twisting her fingers in her lap. Ever since Nash's brother had found her unconscious with her baby in his barn, Hope had been on a quest to learn her true identity.

"What did they say?" Ridge asked, immediately on alert.

"They asked if I've seen a woman with long auburn hair, blue eyes and a baby who looks just like her."

"That could be anyone," Ridge said, his eyes darting between Hope and Nash. "Plus, they didn't mention Hope and Evie's matching birthmarks."

"That's right… But if it weren't for the fact that something seemed off about them, I would have told them about Hope."

"But what if they aren't? What if they hold the answers

to my identity?" Hope asked, running her hands through her hair. "What did they look like?"

"They were both average height and looked to be in their late fifties, early sixties. The gentleman was clean-shaven with pepper-gray hair and the woman, whom I assume is his wife, had blond, shoulder-length hair. They were both neatly dressed and drove a station wagon."

Hope closed her eyes and rubbed her temples. "I have flashes of memory with a middle-aged couple. I can see them holding out their arms, and at first, they seem kind, but then their faces and voices turn angry…" She shook her head and slumped. "That's all I've got."

"It's okay," Ridge soothed, reaching to take her hand.

Goose bumps popped up on Nash's arms. He had a sinking feeling that the couple he had met earlier was the same couple from Hope's flashes. Nash wished he had thought to ask them their names. However, if he had done that, the couple would have persisted and he couldn't be sure they meant Hope well.

"Do you think it could be your parents or the paternal grandparents?" Imani asked, her tone empathetic. She moved to Hope's side.

Hope lifted her shoulders, then sighed. "I have no idea."

"I could see if the cameras picked up on their license plates and we could investigate," Nash offered.

"Ooh, that's a good idea!" Imani chimed in, scooting to the edge of the love seat.

But Ridge lifted a hand and shook his head. "I think the best recourse is for us to wait. We need Hope's memories to return before we do anything."

Nash could see how much Ridge cared for Hope and he wondered if his younger brother was afraid of Hope finding out the truth about who she was, then possibly leaving him. After all, for all they knew, Hope could be a married woman.

Jumping to his feet, Nash went to get some water. From where he stood in the kitchen, he studied Imani chatting with Hope and his brother looking at Hope with such devotion. Such certainty. His gut twisted.

Months ago, he had let Imani go without too much of a fight because she wanted to be a parent. Meanwhile, he was pretty sure that Ridge would trade places with him faster than he could snap his fingers. His brother had taken to fatherhood like a horse to carrots and he would love to have a real relationship with Hope.

His brother's plight strengthened Nash's resolve. He needed to up his game. Be the best father he could for Colt. Imani's eyes met his. She gave him a shy smile. And he needed to hold on to Imani with all his might.

Evie cried out. "I'll go check on her," Hope said, getting to her feet. Ridge was right behind her.

Returning to where Imani sat, Nash held out a hand and pulled her to stand. He gave her a quick, passionate kiss. Tenderly, he ran his hands through her curls, before touching her cheek.

Her eyes narrowed. "Are you alright?"

"Never better. I'd love to take you out on a real date."

"A *real* date?" Imani repeated, her brown eyes warm and inviting.

Gosh, she was beautiful. She took his breath away. Nash nodded. "Yes, and before you ask, I can think of the perfect pint-size chaperone."

Chapter Nineteen

The next evening around six thirty, Imani left the guest-house to meet Nash on his boat down by the water, or more accurately, on his cabin cruiser. He had already gone ahead with Colt to get everything prepared. She had strict orders to wait twenty-five minutes before venturing down to the dock.

Imani fretted with her hair, which she had pinned in a messy bun, while she made her way down the path. Nash had said to dress casually so she had chosen a cardigan set and white jeans. She walked down the ramp and gave him a wave.

Colt was in his swing under the awning. Imani hadn't noticed Nash leaving the house with it but that was a good idea.

As he helped her onto his cruiser, she asked, "Are we going out on the water?"

"No, we're on this vessel strictly for the ambience." Nash gave her a wide smile and tipped his cowboy hat. He had on a sweater and a pair of white shorts along with loafers.

She placed a hand on her chest, unable to hide her relief. It was a warm night out and Colt was dressed in a sweater set, under his blanket, but she feared him catching a draft. Imani didn't want to deal with a sick infant anytime soon.

She would say not at all, but she knew that wish would be unrealistic.

Underneath the awning was a built-in table and seating. On the table, Nash had laid out what appeared to be sandwiches, fruit and—she sniffed—chicken noodle soup, if her nose was to be believed. There was sparkling cider cooling in an ice bucket with three wineglasses she assumed were plastic. The good thing was everything was disposable, so there wouldn't be any lengthy cleanup needed. Next to Colt's swing, there were three sets of canvases on easels and paint supplies.

"What's this about?" She snorted. "I know Colt isn't about to pick up that paintbrush."

"You'll see." He winked at her before extending a hand toward the food. "Are you ready to eat?"

"For sure." She rubbed her tummy.

Ever the perfect gentleman, he took her hand in his and gestured for her to take a seat. Then he slipped in beside her. Everywhere their bodies touched, she felt electric impulses. Her body hummed because of their proximity. While they ate, Nash leaned over to kiss her cheeks and played with the tendrils of her hair at the base of her neck.

"Hello?" a voice called out just as they finished eating.

"We're over here." Nash popped up to greet the newest arrival. Imani tossed their refuse in the trash.

A young woman dressed in all black appeared, her apron covered with pictures of paintbrushes. Nash made quick introductions. "Tonight, we are going to sip sparkling cider and paint, following Alana's directions."

Alana sported an afro with supersize earrings that swayed with the tiniest of movement. "We are going to paint the sunset over the water. I will guide you each step of the way."

Imani's eyebrows rose and she addressed Nash. "I'm impressed."

He bowed. "I aim to please."

Alana began with the blue paint and by starting the outline in the middle of the canvas. Imani and Nash did the same. The gentle sway of the boat and the dipping sun became the perfect backdrop for their scene. With each stroke of the brush, step by step, they created similar images, then they each added personalized details with Alana's guidance. Nash also used every free opportunity to touch her, kiss her, play with her hair. Not to be outdone, Imani's hands had been busy, too. Their playfulness left them with paint in their hair, on their noses and their clothes.

Colt slept the entire ninety minutes of their date. Talk about perfect planning. That and the fact that he drank close to two ounces of formula.

Once their painting session was over and Alana had departed, Imani wrapped the baby about her and took the small bag of trash, while Nash took the swing and the paintings.

"This was a marvelous date," she breathed out, as they traipsed back to the guesthouse. "From start to end, I can't tell when I've had a more enjoyable time. Thank you, Nash."

"You're welcome." His chest puffed. "I have Google to thank, though. I believe my search words were *dates for parents with a newborn*."

"Oh?" Her brow arched. "What else did they suggest?"

"Walks, board games, visiting a farm, the beach…stuff like that."

"I like that." She smiled. Her heart warmed at his thoughtfulness. And she appreciated that he had researched things they could do with the baby around. They arrived outside the guesthouse and the sensor lights came on. After putting down the swing, Nash opened the door.

She tilted her head back and took in the glorious feel of the crisp fall wind in her hair and the back of her neck. "What a beautiful night."

"What a beautiful woman," he murmured. His eyes glinted in the moonlight. She shivered and it had nothing to do with the temperature and everything to do with the man slaking his eyes down the length of her body.

"Soon," she whispered.

He pinned her with his fiery gaze. "I'll hold you to that."

Stepping past the threshold ahead of him, she could feel his eyes on her butt. Once inside, Imani handed Nash the trash and rested Colt in his bassinet in her bedroom. He didn't even stir. It was a little after 8:00 p.m. She ran her hands through her hair. Ugh. She needed to throw these clothes in the wash and take a long, hot shower.

She said as much to Nash when he entered the room. There was a streak of blue paint across his cheekbone. "Why don't I join you?" he suggested.

"The shower can fit the both of us but it will be a tight squeeze."

"That'll work for me," he said, his voice husky.

"Alright. Just don't drop the soap," she teased.

He smirked. "Oh, please do…"

Imani slipped her shirt off her head and wiggled out of her jeans with Nash eyeing her every move. She tossed them in the hamper and sauntered into the bathroom, making sure to grab the baby monitor. The bathroom was done in white with chrome trimmings. Meanwhile the floor, counter space and tiles were all marble. Though each had variations of the design. The mats and towels were a deep chocolate-brown. Turning on the spigot of the walk-in shower, she tested the water. Ahh. Nice and hot. She walked under the spray, running her hands through her hair. Nash entered behind her, his gaze lustful and wanting.

It had been a minute since she had seen him naked. She took her time reacquainting herself with those wide shoulders, that broad chest, his taut, tight stomach muscles and his engorged member. *Oh, my.* The space in the shower suddenly felt smaller. She was so aware of this man—he sucked up all her space.

Nash was also checking her out.

"I have stretch marks," she pointed out, when she saw his eyes on her tummy.

"They humble me," he said quietly, reaching out to touch her abdomen. "Thank you for my son."

Imani busied herself with lathering her body before pumping a handful of shampoo to massage her hair. Nash did the same. Then he washed her back and she washed his, their bodies touching this way and that. A bump here, a graze there, made for a sensual experience that left them both wanting, hungry for more than food.

They used their lips and hands to provide pleasure, stoking the fire within her that he did his best to quench. Imani took care of Nash, though. His satisfying grunt signaled the end of their shower.

Engulfed in a warm, fluffy towel, she dried her hair. "Thank you for an amazing time from beginning to end," she murmured, her heart light.

"The night's not done yet," Nash said, snuggling close to her, his towel wrapped around his waist.

Colt's wail came through the monitor. On cue. "You're right." She laughed. "It sure isn't."

He gave her a quick kiss and squeezed her shoulder.

"Finish up here. I'll go get him." Watching his departure, Imani concluded that his confident swagger as he left to care for their son was by far the sexiest thing she had seen all night.

Chapter Twenty

Colt had gained two pounds and he had even grown an inch. Nash whooped when he heard that. Imani practically skipped out of the doctor's office.

She was winning at motherhood.

And she was also winning at rebuilding her relationship with Nash.

The past few days with Nash had been nothing short of marvelous. He had been a model parent…and partner. Their dates consisted of walks around the lake with long talks, while eating corn dogs or ice cream. All of which continued to draw her closer to him. Her heart rate accelerated when she was in his presence and Imani was enjoying the rush.

After waving off Nash, who had started his morning very early at the ranch, she buckled Colt into his car seat and began her trek back to the guesthouse.

Imani also credited her sessions with a mental-health professional who specialized in working with new mothers for her renewed optimism. Her therapist had suggested she purchase a journal, and who knew? Journaling helped.

That's why this evening, she was surprising Nash by taking him up on his offer of visiting his beloved horses. She couldn't ride until she was about six to eight weeks postpartum, but she figured this was the next best thing.

Besides, she knew this would make Nash happy. A lot of his talks with her revolved around ranching.

But she was going without Colt.

Her stomach knotted a wee bit at that, but she was determined to push through. Her mother and grandmother were back at the resort, and would be coming over to babysit. Abena had been overjoyed when she heard her intentions.

Imani had also extended an invite to Wendy, who was more than happy to reconnect with Imani's family and see her grandson.

She had used a personal stylist, and settled on a faux suede fringe jacket, a button-down top, denim leggings and Italian cowgirl boots for this excursion. As soon as her mother and grandma arrived, Imani rushed to get dressed. She completed her look with a little bronzer, eyeliner and ruby-red lipstick. Nash was due to arrive home in about ten minutes.

"You look stunning," Abena said, eyeing her from head to toe.

"Yes, have you been exercising?" Zuri asked.

"Nash and I have been walking the expanse of the lake, but it's only been a few days," Imani said. "I think Colt's going to love the outdoors. Just like his daddy."

Her mom arched an eyebrow. "So I take it Nash has finally embraced fatherhood?"

"I think so. Although, I feel like he is still wary of staying with Colt on his own for an extended period of time. The day Nia and I went to the spa, he told me he went by his mother's house not too long after I left." She didn't mention her panic attack when she discovered Nash wasn't there. "I don't think Nash trusts himself around a newborn so I suspect he just wanted someone else around—just in case."

"I get that, but a part of bonding is spending that one-on-one quality time with your child," Zuri chimed in. "I did that with Phillip and I made Hammond do the same." She chuckled. "His first time alone with Phillip was pretty memorable."

"What happened?" Abena asked, her face alight with fascination.

Imani smiled. She loved when her grandma shared stories of her dad. "Yes, do tell. Inquiring minds want to know!"

Zuri's skin tinted crimson. "Well, when Hammond fell asleep, Phillip had a bowel movement in his crib. I don't know what Hammond fed him. I still don't know. I'll be delicate and say, we spent the next three hours cleaning the baby, the blanket and the crib." Her shoulders shook with mirth.

Imani's eyes went wide before she and Abena dissolved into laughter.

"Whoa. That was hilarious. I'll never look at Dad the same." She glanced at her mother. "Do you have stories like that of me?"

"No, dear. You were my little angel," Abena said, then shook her head. "Jonathan, however, was a different story. I couldn't take my eyes off him. He was a climber. Whenever he went missing, I would always have to look up because that little stinker would be in the cupboard, at the top of the curtains. Problem was, he didn't know how to come back down."

"Yes, that boy was a handful. I'll never forget when your father called to tell me they caught Jonathan sitting in the fish tank grabbing after them," Zuri added. "The only reason they found him is because you were standing there crying and begging him not to kill the fishies."

Another round of laughter followed.

Her grandmother scrunched her nose. "I'm pretty sure

I have a picture of it somewhere. I've got to search my albums."

"I'd love to see those." Imani dabbed at her eyes. "I look forward to Nash and I having stories like these to reminisce of Colt one day."

"Well, they weren't funny at the time," Abena said. "But they do make for heartwarming memories."

Imani ran her index finger down the bridge of her nose. "Maybe all us women need to go out to give Nash alone time with Colt. It might boost his confidence once he gets through it."

"How about tomorrow morning?" Zuri suggested. "We can go for an early morning walk and then head over to the LC Club."

Abena's eyes flashed. "I like that idea."

Imani placed a hand across her tummy. She hadn't expected to put their plan in action the very next day. But there wasn't any reason not to…

The lock clicked.

"Let us know before we leave," Abena whispered. "I'm in."

Wendy came in, followed by Nash. They must have arrived at the same time. "Look who's paying us a visit," Nash said.

A round of greetings and hugs ensued. Nash's eyes slaked her body with barely banked passion, flaring her own. "You look nice." He emphasized the word *nice* in a way that made Imani blush. He had on a cowboy hat, and a checkered shirt tucked into a pair of jeans that appeared to be tailor-made. "Going somewhere?"

She lowered her lashes. "Yes, I'm going out to dinner with you," she said breathily. "It's my turn to plan a special date."

He leaned in. "Out, as in leaving this house?"

"Mmm-hmm." She nodded as she smiled, even as her heart rate escalated. "Our mothers agreed to babysit."

His lips widened into a slow, sexy smile. "Where do you have planned?"

Those cognac eyes of his made her tummy dance like a jitterbug. "I figure I could meet Onyx or Leviathan today, and then we grab a quick bite afterward at the diner."

"Really? You want to go to the ranch?" He gave her a quick hug. "I didn't think you could ride again yet."

"I can't, but I can watch you do your thing so I can scratch *date with a hot rancher* off my bucket list," she teased, giving him a once-over and fanning herself.

Her grandmother snickered. "Watch yourself, now. That's how you ended up pregnant the first time."

"Yeah, you both made a cute baby together," her mother said. "But still…"

"Ah, you two need to get going," Wendy chimed in. "The diner won't be open much longer. Small town." She shooed them toward the door.

"Alright. We'd better go," Imani agreed, before rushing into the nursery to give Colt a kiss on his forehead. "Mommy will be back soon," she whispered. After slinging her backpack over her shoulder, she joined hands with Nash before she stepped outside. As soon as the door closed behind them, Nash whipped her around and kissed her with urgency. Imani moaned, grabbing the back of his head as their tongues engaged in a tug-of-war.

"I've been thinking about doing this all day," Nash said, his chest heaving.

"Less thinking and more doing." Imani brought him in for another searing kiss.

Needless to say, during the short car ride to the ranch, raw tension crackled between them along with…frustration. Oh, how she wished she could cool down this heat with some no-holds-barred lovemaking.

Whew. November 28th couldn't come fast enough. Thanksgiving. And oh, how she planned on giving thanks that day.

She could feel Nash's eyes on her rear. Like lasers. Swinging her hips, Imani decided to give him a show, smiling with satisfaction at his groan. She entered the stables first. Since the workers were finished for the day, the two of them were the sole human occupants inside.

Perfect.

It was time to check off another bucket-list item.

Nash took her to the first stall, standing on the left. Holding her hand, he introduced her to Onyx first, then Leviathan and Midnight. Imani marveled at the strength and beauty of each horse. All three horses were gorgeous black thoroughbreds. Nash was so patient, stroking their manes and talking to them, and it was evident how much he loved these animals. They followed him with their eyes. The affection between man and beast was mutual. Her heart warmed.

Next, Nash got on the saddle and showed off some of his riding skills with Midnight. Which meant she had to take her camera out because, talk about hot. He sure looked good with that cowboy hat.

"I'm so glad you're doing what you love," she said, linking her arm through his once he was finished. "For many, that's a luxury."

"I know I'm blessed I have the means to make my passion my work."

She got on her tiptoes to give him a peck on the cheek. "But I would love to see your other riding skills."

Her low, throaty spoken words caused his eyebrows to raise. "Now you know you wrong for trying to be flirty right now when there's nothing I can do about it."

"I know, but as you see when we showered, we can be creative..." She let the suggestion hang between them, hiding her smile.

Nash stepped back. "Easy now... I'll be back in a minute. Let me go to wash up a little before we go to dinner." He strutted out of the barn like he knew she had her eyes on him. Which she did.

As soon as he was out of sight, she dug into her backpack and took out the cowgirl lingerie featuring a long-sleeved fringe bodysuit with garter straps. She shimmied into the mesh stockings before slipping into thigh-high black boots. They couldn't sleep together but she could give him an appetizer, something to look forward to. Gosh, her hands were shaking and her palms were sweaty but she got everything on without ripping the scraps of material. It was a good thing it was warm in the barn.

Once she was dressed, she jumped on top of the bale of hay and settled into a seductive pose.

She hoped Nash appreciated her efforts. Because her butt itched, and hay was all in her hair. She gritted her teeth to keep from scratching. Dang. Why hadn't she brought a blanket?

She heard a whistle before Nash rounded the corner. He dashed toward where she was and looked down at her. "Whoa." The look of hunger on his face was worth every discomfort. His mouth opened and closed, then opened and closed again.

It wasn't often she saw Nash Fortune speechless.

She licked her lips and recited the line she had practiced

in her head countless times. "Do you prefer your cowgirls naughty or nice?"

He dropped to his knees and responded with an intriguing question of his own. "How about a little of both?"

Chapter Twenty-One

He loved his mother. Dearly. But Nash wished she would leave and take Imani's folks right along with her. He was ready to continue what he and Imani had started in the barn. It was like only having one scoop of ice cream.

But the women were watching a movie about a book club and they were only halfway through. He loved how both his and Imani's families blended well together. At one point, his mom and Abena had been huddled in the corner, conspiring together about something.

Nash sat in the armchair with his hat over his eyes so he could trail Imani's every move. He was aware of every step and every breath she took. That's how tuned into her he was. She held Colt, rocking him back and forth. But all Nash could think about was the fact that she was still wearing that scrap of lingerie underneath.

He still couldn't believe Imani had been daring enough to pull that stunt in the barn. She had done things to him that were so naughty, but oh, so nice. Seared in his memory for life was when she flipped onto her tummy, then asked the most enticing question he had ever heard: *Why don't you get your camera out?*

Nash had gone along with her cheeky suggestion, snapping a few pictures, but he had every intention of deleting them all after their fun time. However, Imani urged him to store them in a photo-lock app. And, of course, she had taken a few pictures of him. *For later*, she had said with a mischievous giggle.

He had indulged her whimsy, while warning her they were for her eyes only. It was the twinkle in her eyes he was low-key worried about. Nash didn't need her boasting of his assets to anyone. As soon as they were able to make love, Nash planned to clear the photos out of both their phones. She didn't need a still when she had access to the real thing.

Though he had to admit that Imani had fulfilled one of his teenage fantasies. And then some. He would never be able to enter that barn without thinking of her again. It had taken every ounce of willpower he possessed not to sink into her while she was on that bale with her leg propped up. But he wasn't about to cause her harm because he couldn't wait.

Besides, as Imani said, they had gotten creative. *Real creative*.

Colt's cries made him focus on the present. Imani's curls looked wild, bouncing as she rocked the baby—patience had been needed to remove the hay from her hair. But to Nash, she had never looked more beautiful. She had showered and changed when they returned from their date before getting Colt out of his bassinet.

He jumped to his feet and went over to take his son from her. "I've got this," he said, his stomach rumbling. They had been so caught up in each other that they hadn't eaten dinner.

Her lips quirked. "Let's get Colt fed first and we can eat after."

"Yes, because you were wrong, you know?" he said under his breath.

"Wrong about what?"

"We can't live off love," he rasped, repeating the words Imani had voiced when Nash reminded her that the diner was about to close while they were fooling around in the barn. "A man's got to eat."

She winked. "I've ordered special delivery from the LC Club. It should arrive shortly."

They high-fived. "Now, that's what I'm talking about." Colt squirmed against him then opened his mouth like he was trying to eat Nash's shirt. Oh, no. He should have gotten a receiving blanket. Holding Colt a few inches from him, he went to get one and slung it across his chest.

Imani returned with Colt's bottle and Nash returned to the armchair to feed his son. Colt's hair looked even more curly and his lashes touched his cheeks. He could see the dimple on display every time Colt sucked his cheeks in. "I love you," he whispered. Less than five minutes later, Colt had finished his bottle. His son had a healthy appetite.

Nash sat the baby up and patted his back. Colt burped soon after. Nash felt adept at feeding him, though he still hadn't mastered changing his son's diaper. The day he was watching him by himself, Nash had tried three times and each time, there was a gap big enough so that the diaper had slipped off Colt's legs. That's why he had gone to his mother's house.

Imani came over with the baby wrap sling for him to use. She kissed the top of Colt's head and then did the same to Nash.

His heart somersaulted.

This woman was the whole package.

That's why he loved her.

Yes, he loved her. Acknowledging the feeling blossoming within his chest was that easy, like crossing home plate after hitting a home run. He didn't have any angst or need to agonize over how he felt about Imani.

Nash stood surrounded by noise—the mothers laughing at the screen, Imani talking with the delivery guy at the door, Zuri lightly snoring—and all he could hear was the quiet certainty of his heart.

He knew he would spend the rest of his days with this woman. If she would have him. He loved her and he had a hunch that he would continually fall into that abyss with a smile on his face.

Imani sauntered over, holding up the paper bag bearing the LC Club logo. "Dinner is served." *She was a provider.* He fell a little more.

Abena paused the television. "I hope you ordered enough for all of us. I know I ate earlier but I could eat."

"I sure did," Imani said.

She was thoughtful. He fell even deeper.

Washing her hands, Imani addressed Wendy. "Oh, before I forget, remind me to give you the monogrammed onesies. I also had a special set made for Dahlia's twins."

"Oh, wow. Thank you. How sweet."

She was kind. And there he was falling for her all over again.

Wendy came over to assist Imani with laying out the spread. He must have an incredulous look on his face or something because she tilted her head. "Are you okay?"

"Oh, yes. I've never been better."

"Just checking because you spilled some of the gravy all over the baby bag." Nash looked down to see the liquid seeping down the sides and soiling the contents inside. Mortified, he took out the clothes and diapers to inspect them.

"Don't worry about it," Imani said. "I'll wash the clothes and repack the bag later. Go eat." She quickly wiped out the bag with bleached wipes and chucked the diapers in the trash.

"If you're sure…"

"Positive." After their meal, Imani joined the women to finish the last half hour of the film.

Nash wandered over to the kitchen counter, where Imani had placed the real-estate agent's contact information along with several listings. She was in the investigation stage but as soon as Colt was two months, Imani would start house hunting in earnest. Her ideal home would have at least six bedrooms, a large office area, a spacious nursery and enough acreage for her to have a playground, a pool, a tennis court, a trail and, of course, a privacy fence. Imani's intention was to close on a property in time to move in at the four-month mark.

Hopefully, his love and offer of a more permanent living situation would change her mind. And what better day to express how thankful he was that she had returned into his life and captured his heart, than on Thanksgiving?

A faint cry awakened him.

Stretched across the bed in Imani's room the Monday of Thanksgiving week, it took a moment for Nash to register where he was and that he was hearing Colt crying from the baby monitor. He propped himself up on his elbows before zeroing on a note on the side of the bed.

Left early to go with our mothers on a walk. Be back soon.

He tensed. That meant he was alone with Colt. On one hand, Nash was glad Imani was overcoming her separation anxiety. But on the other…he was alone with his son.

The cries became more persistent. It was six in the morning, which meant Colt had slept for a good six hours. The baby wasn't going back to bed. It was feeding time. Nash swung his legs off the side of the bed and rushed into the nursery. Colt was now in full wail, his fists bunched and his face scrunched. Nash picked up his child and held him close to rock him.

"Okay, okay, Daddy's here." Colt hiccupped, his chin trembling. Swaying from side to side, Nash felt a little heat radiating from the infant's back. He frowned. Actually, Colt felt *really* warm. Maybe he had overheated from his crying bout. Placing him in the bassinet, Nash reached for a diaper. Colt started fussing again. What should he do? Change him or pick him up? Nash wiped his forehead with the back of his hand and attempted to ignore the panic rising within. Colt stiffened and his face reddened. Uh-oh. He knew what was coming.

Colt bellowed.

Maybe he was hungry. Man, this felt easier to navigate when Imani was around. Nash bolted into the kitchen and grabbed a bottle out of the bottle sanitizer. Thank goodness, Imani had made him wash them all the night before. Colt was now having a major meltdown.

Snatching the baby in his arms, Nash tried to give him a bottle, but Colt refused. In fact, he seemed to be really congested and was grunting, and now his hiccups had gotten worse.

Nash's chest heaved. He hated seeing his baby boy so upset. Helplessness threatened to engulf him, but he gave himself a pep talk. "Okay, Nash, you can do this. You've been doing it for the past three weeks. This is nothing new." Then he tried again. This time, Colt latched on and began sucking away. The whizzing sound of the milk made Nash heave a sigh of relief. "Alright, little guy. Fill your tummy."

Then Colt hiccupped while feeding. Nash took the bottle out of Colt's mouth and scrambled to set him upright. Colt began to heave, spitting up all the milk he had consumed. Nash grabbed some napkins and wiped the baby's face, then patted his back, but he just got fussier.

Nash paused. He hadn't changed Colt's diaper yet, which could be the cause of his unease. Poor little guy couldn't talk about what was bothering him. Nash rested him on his back and took off his diaper. He gasped. Was it him or did Colt's skin seem flushed? Nash moved with speed to wipe his son down and apply some ointment, the way he had seen Imani do. Then he put him in a fresh diaper, tightly securing the sides. Lifting the baby up, Nash exhaled when it stayed on.

Colt was silent for a blessed three seconds. Then he arched his back and screamed.

Nash stilled.

This was *not* normal.

He had to get Colt to the pediatrician's office. He put his boy back into the bassinet before speeding into action. First, he dialed the doctor's office, yelling above the infant's screams, and almost cried when they told him he could bring Colt in. Nash's heart pounded as he grabbed the baby bag. Then, he tossed some diapers inside and checked to see if there were wipes inside, then raced outside the house.

Colt's screams pierced Nash's ears and his heart.

On the way to the doctor, he called Imani to let her know he was on the way to the pediatrician.

"Does he have a fever?" Imani asked, her tone frantic.

"I—I don't know…"

"You didn't check?" Maybe he was being sensitive but her tone sounded accusatory. That put him on the defensive.

"N-no. I was busy trying to feed him and change him and he's crying and throwing up. I—I just don't know…"

"There's a thermometer in Colt's bathroom. All you had to do was check." Nash slumped. He could hear their mothers trying to calm Imani down. Nash understood her fears, but she wasn't the only one scared. In the back seat of his Range Rover, Colt was inconsolable. Nash groaned.

"I didn't think. I'm sorry. Colt is screaming and I panicked. I told you I wasn't good at this, and you left me to look after him by myself," he said, lashing out.

"I'm just asking you what anybody would know… I shouldn't have left him behind to go walking." *Wow. So Imani really didn't actually trust him alone with their son.* That gutted his heart. Yes, he had his doubts about his capabilities, but he did his best to be helpful and to assist with Colt however he could. As Nash tried to process her words, she grunted out, "I'll see you at the doctor's office." Then the line went dead.

Chapter Twenty-Two

"Keep calm," Abena said, patting Imani's hand. "Don't get yourself worked up until you know what's going on." They had met up by the lake at five that morning and had just finished one lap around the circumference when Nash called.

How was she to stay cool with Colt screaming like he was in pain? This idea of theirs to leave Nash alone with the baby had backfired big-time. Instead of helping him gain confidence in his parenting skills, it only made Imani acutely aware of what she was lacking in hers. Regret filled her gut, twisted it tighter than a Bantu knot. Fighting back tears, Imani prayed her baby was okay.

She shouldn't have relaxed her routine and left Nash to take care of Colt. She could have strapped her baby boy into the stroller and taken him on her walk. A cloak of guilt wrapped around her. No. No. She couldn't think like that. What was happening to Colt would happen if she'd been there or not and it had nothing to do with her negligence. She had left him with his father.

The very father who now blamed her for Colt getting sick.

Her stomach churned with that knowledge.

The women hurried toward Imani's car. Imani handed

her mother the keys. She was too shaky to get behind the wheel.

"Take deep breaths. All will be fine," Wendy said, with the cool manner of one who had reared six children. She didn't sound alarmed and Imani drew from that and tried to quell her body quivers. All she could hear were Colt's screams. All she could feel was her self-reproach.

"How was Colt last night?" Wendy asked.

Imani narrowed her eyes, picturing Colt the night before. "He seemed okay. Slept well. Got up about eleven and stayed up until about one in the morning. I didn't notice anything wrong." Or had she missed something?

"It might be colic," Zuri added, tapping her chin. "If I remember right, of my three girls, Abena used to get colic all the time. You don't know how many nights I stayed up massaging her tummy and trying to get her settled."

Just as they pulled into the parking lot of the medical building, Nash texted. I am here. They are taking Colt back now.

Tossing her phone in her purse, Imani jumped out of the vehicle and rushed inside the building. "Keep us posted," her mother called out.

She caught up with Nash as they were being led into Exam Room 2. Colt wasn't screaming but he was sniffling. Seeing his puffy face made her heart ache. She stood back while the nurse's assistant took Colt's temperature and his weight. He didn't have a fever, thank goodness. And he hadn't lost any weight.

Without meeting Nash's gaze, Imani held out her hands. He handed Colt over to her and though she could feel Nash's eyes on her, she didn't acknowledge him. She was too upset at him for blaming her for leaving Colt with him. As if he was a stranger. Colt snuggled into her and yawned. Poor baby wanted to sleep. Sitting in one of two free chairs, she massaged the baby's tummy. Colt began passing wind.

"Are you upset with me?" Nash asked.

"Yes." She spoke through clenched teeth.

"I'm sorry I didn't think to check his temperature."

"I'm not upset about that."

He furrowed his brow in confusion. "Then what did I do?"

The door creaked. "We'll talk later." The pediatrician entered with his assistant. Within minutes of his examination, he diagnosed Colt was colic, suggesting that they change the formula.

"What brand does he use?" the physician asked.

"Let me show you a sample," Imani said, opening the diaper bag. "We've used two different kinds." She rummaged around the interior but all she saw were diapers and baby wipes. There wasn't even a change of clothes.

"Ugh. I—I must have forgotten to pack the formula," Nash slapped his forehead.

The doctor must have sensed the tension between them because he jumped in before Imani could speak. "That's okay. I have a couple of samples for a gentler formula that you can try. Your baby's digestive tract isn't fully mature yet and so he could be getting used to the shift."

By then Colt had finally fallen asleep. The pediatrician gave them at least six small bottles and promised to call them in a few days to check on Colt. Placing Colt on her shoulder, Imani thanked the doctor, then left the building ahead of Nash. She had every intention of taking the baby into her vehicle, but her Jeep was gone. So she had to ride back to the guesthouse with Nash.

Imani surmised their mothers had driven off to give the two of them space to talk, which now that she thought about it, was a good thing. She wasn't going to walk around with her chest tight from all these emotions.

Once they had Colt secured and Nash was on his way, she cleared her throat. "I didn't appreciate you coming at me for going on a walk with our mothers this morning. In these past twenty-one days, I have barely left my son's side. In fact, the only time I did was because you suggested it. I'm not a neglectful mother so for you to imply that was below the belt, especially since I was gone for about an hour."

Nash's mouth popped open. "When did I say that? I think you are an amazing mother and I'm glad when you take time for yourself. I was the one who talked about balance, remember?"

"Yes, but you blamed me for leaving Colt with you." She folded her arms.

He shook his head. "You misunderstood what I meant. You have a natural instinct when it comes to Colt and this morning proved that. I'm woefully unequipped to deal with a newborn on my own. I'm just like my father."

"You are nothing like the man you described," Imani replied vehemently. "Every day you tell Colt how much you love him and you have been there. Why are you letting a couple mistakes interfere with the overall picture?"

He tossed a meaningful glance her way. She shifted in her seat. "I get that I'm doing the same thing but the difference between you and me is that I am trying to work through my doubts. I'm not going to let anxiety get in the way of my giving Colt what he needs."

"Our son doesn't need a father who doesn't think to check his temperature, or one who leaves the house without thinking about how he is going to eat."

She placed a hand on Nash's arm. "We're going to make mistakes. The main thing is that we love Colt."

"Yes, but some are forgivable. And I do love Colt. That's why I know I need to stay away from him if he's ever going to turn out right."

"I can't believe you would even say something like that. If you cut him out of your life, you're causing the same trauma you experienced as a child."

His eyes widened. "Negative. I'm sparing him from similar trauma." He parked in front of the guesthouse. "My being in his life could bring him more harm than good. It's in my blood."

"Some of your siblings became parents and they are coping well. You will, too, in time."

"That's them." He pointed to his chest. "This is me."

She sighed. "I can see that no matter what I say, you've made up your mind." Tears welled. "How am I to explain to Colt when he asks why he doesn't have his father in his life?"

"When he's older, I'll explain it to him."

She lifted her chin. "And what if he doesn't want to hear a word you have to say?"

Nash looked her square in the eyes. "I'm willing to take that chance."

Her shoulders slumped. "I see." She placed her hand on the door handle. "Then I guess there's nothing left to say."

I'm willing to take that chance.

Three hours after he had spoken those words, Imani and Colt were gone. She must have called a moving company and hired a cleaning crew to remove all signs of their occupancy. Everything was the way it had been before. Immaculate. Pristine… Quiet.

He hated it.

After their talk, Nash had gone to the ranch to work and

to give Imani some space. But he had missed them and had returned home, scrambling immediately toward the guesthouse. Walking through the empty space, his footsteps echoed throughout, a cloud of loneliness shrouding his every move. The nursery had been completely dismantled, like she had been trying to erase any evidence of Colt's existence.

Imani hadn't even left a note or a forwarding address so he had no idea if she had returned to Cactus Grove or if she was still in Chatelaine Hills.

He fired off a rapid text to Imani. I can't believe you left like that.

Her response was quick. I can't believe you would think I would stay.

Despondent at her comeback, Nash walked the path back to his home. Flipping on the switch, he thought about taking his Jaguar out on the road. But when he went into the garage, the vivid image of Imani relaxing against the seat, her curls flying in the wind, made him retreat.

He ran his hand across the hood. "Sorry, Velvet. Maybe another time."

Puttering around his house, Nash wiped the already clean counters and dusted the fans, but there wasn't much to do. Not even Taylor Swift helped. Talking to his mother about it hadn't helped, either. When the silence became overbearing, he drove back to the ranch. He would visit with his horses and fill their stalls with fresh hay. He doubted they would need it but it would fill the void left by Imani and Colt's sudden departure. The tents were already laid out on the field for the Thanksgiving feast Wendy had arranged for the workers. And the party supplier would lay out the tables and chairs soon. Their staff had been delighted at Wendy's gesture.

Going into the barn, memories of his visit there with Imani filled him with melancholy. At dusk, he took Leviathan for a ride when he thought he saw his mother in the distance. Nash was about to trot her way when he saw a man approach. They were far enough away that he couldn't make out any features but they seemed to be deep in conversation.

"Whoa." He cued the horse to stop. Leaning forward in the saddle, he squinted. Wait. Was his mom dating someone? That was…interesting.

Nash straightened, then smiled. He hoped so. Mom had been lonely for a long time, even before his father's death a year ago. It would be good if she had found a new partner, a second chance at love. Especially since she had been encouraging all of her children to do the same. The two people strolled away from him, arm in arm.

Leviathan whinnied, lifting his legs, restless. "Steady. Steady," he commanded gently. His horse snorted. Nash used his left leg to give the horse a squeeze and tilted his head and shoulders to the right. The horse turned and they trotted back to the stable. After placing Leviathan in his stall, he went outside to take in the glow of the full moon. Seeing his mother with someone magnified Nash's sudden solitude.

The next seventy-two hours were excruciating. Nash awakened at odd hours, thinking he had heard Colt's cry. He sent Imani text messages and called a few times but she didn't respond. Battling insomnia, he did some work inside his house, his heart aching for Imani's company. Her voice. Her touch. Nash bunched his fists. This was what he wanted, so why was he feeling so…on edge? Especially when he knew he had made the right decision. Colt would be better off without him.

But he hadn't been without his father. Yet, he was hoping for a different outcome with his son when he was doing the same thing to Colt that Casper had done to him.

Nash didn't feel good about that.

Chapter Twenty-Three

Thanksgiving Day, Nash started his day early, having spent most of the night tossing and turning in bed. He went over to the ranch to help with last-minute setup and to thank the workers for all their hard work. He also promoted Stanley to full-time status. Seeing Stanley's wife and daughter cheer for his accomplishment made Nash think of Imani and Colt.

When Imani and Nash parted ways before, it had been difficult to move on, but it had been doable. However, this time, his heart felt ripped to shreds, the pain doubly intensified. He couldn't sleep, his appetite deserted him and regret ate at him. He missed Imani's voice, her laugh, her touch. The feel of his son in his arms, the look of trust on Colt's face. And, more than anything, he missed telling his son he loved him every day.

His dour mood was in direct contrast to the festive music, and though he had planted a smile on his face, his heart was heavy. Being here without Imani and Colt was a struggle.

Wendy came over to where he stood by the side of the tent. She handed him a cup of apple cider. "How are things with Imani?"

"I haven't spoken to her in days," he croaked out. "The silence is interminable."

"Oh, son. I'm sorry to see you like this. But have you learned anything?"

"Yes, I know I'm miserable without them. I want Imani and Colt in my life. For always. I want to be there to celebrate Colt's first Christmas. When we were children, I remember how we would gather in the kitchen and bake pies together. I want to continue that tradition with my child."

Wendy chuckled. "I can't believe you remember that. A lot more of the apple slices made it in your mouth than in the pie."

"Yeah, I didn't know you caught that. I figured you would think it was Ridge." His chin dipped to his chest. "I wonder if Colt will like granny apples like I do?"

Instead of answering his question, his mother patted his back. "I really hate to see you suffer, but there is an upside here."

"And what could that possibly be?" Nash grumbled.

"You now see the value of family. Which means you know what to do to fix this."

"You're right... I do. I just hope Imani takes my call this time. I've already tried a few times before, all with no response."

"Only one way to find out." She tilted her head and studied him for a beat before she gave his hand a squeeze. Then with a hum, she wandered off.

Nash took out his phone and called Imani. He needed to hear her voice. But once again, his call went directly to voicemail. His shoulders slumped. If it wasn't for the fact that he knew his siblings would drag him out of the house before they let him spend Thanksgiving alone, Nash would have just gone home to hibernate with his despair. Besides, he had been tasked to bring the pies and he didn't want to shirk that responsibility.

After showering and changing into an orange shirt, black jeans and his black sneakers, Nash arrived at his mother's house after 5:00 p.m. with a couple pies in hand. He parked next to one of the numerous vehicles out front. When he stepped inside his mother's home into the living-room area, Nash greeted Arlo, Ridge and Jade. He did his best to shuck off the blues and gave them each a hug.

"It's about time you got here," Arlo said. "Everybody else is outside."

"Who's everyone?" Nash asked.

"Heath's sisters and ours."

"Mom insisted we wait for you," Ridge added, coming over to grab the pies from Nash. "Let me take these off your hands."

Swerving out of Ridge's reach, Nash chuckled. "Nice try, bro, but Mom would have my head and you know it. That's why she made you bring the juices and water because she knows you would hog the pies." Ridge would eat half of the pies on his own if allowed to. He had such a sweet tooth.

"Whatever. I'll buy my own." Ridge gave him a playful shove. "See you out there."

"Hurry up," Arlo said. "All I had was a PBJ for breakfast, so I'm ready to eat."

Nash gasped when he saw Colt's picture had been added to the family photos on the brandy-colored mantel over the marble fireplace. He went to over to stare at his son's first picture, where he had been swaddled in the hospital blanket. Nash touched his chest. He missed the little guy.

Jade sidled up next to him. "He looks just like you did when you were a baby."

His twin's words made his chest tighten. "Yes, he does."

"If he's anything like you, he'll be remarkable." She gave him a kiss on the cheek.

"I hope he has Imani's spunk, because his father is a coward."

"Ouch. Don't talk about my twin brother like that." Jade's eyes filled with sympathy. "He might be a little pig-headed but he's loyal and he loves hard." She squeezed his arm. "Things will work out as they should."

She sounded so certain, he just had to ask… "How can you be so sure?"

"Look at Heath," Jade said, referring to her fiancé. "What are the odds that after thirty years he would discover then find his long-lost sisters? They grew up apart but now look at them." She pointed to the siblings sitting under the tent with their significant others, along with Charlie, Jade's beloved basset hound. "You would never know they only just met. They are so close."

Nash eyed how they were talking and laughing, and just so…happy. "Their reunion was something, wasn't it?"

"It sure was."

For a little town, Chatelaine had some big secrets and Heath's backstory was just one example. When Heath arrived in Chatelaine, he came with the intention of finding his siblings, the Perry triplets—Tabitha, Lily and Haley—who had each found true love with a Fortune man. With the help of Doris Edwards, an elderly GreatStore employee, who insisted there had been four of them, the Perry sisters and Heath had finally pieced everything together. Heath was born two months before his sisters and they were actually half siblings, as Heath had a different mother. But in addition to finding his sisters, Heath had found Jade.

He had never seen his sister so content. "I'm glad you've found your match."

"Heath's wonderful, thoughtful and he has my back." She had a dreamy look on her face.

"Yes, he was alright with me when he rescued you from that bully, Nina, and agreed to be your fake fiancé." Nash had hated how Nina had picked on his sister when they were in high school. But Jade had held her own and had snagged a good man in the process.

She flashed her ring finger and giggled. "Fake fiancé no more." She held Nash's hand in hers. "You have a chance at the real thing, too."

"I think I blew it with Imani. For good this time." Nash gave her a quick rundown of what had happened.

"You can fix it. Just let your heart lead you." How he wished he had his twin's confidence. Her cell phone chimed. "Heath needs barbecue sauce."

"Go on. I'll be out in a second."

Strolling into the kitchen, Nash placed the pies on the island. The entire expanse of the white marble counter was covered with covered foiled containers. He inhaled, the scents of turkey and roast beef filling his nostrils. Wendy had set up burners under the tent in the back of the house, which overlooked the lake and multileveled deck and patio.

Peering outside, Nash could see Heath was by the grill, tending to the chicken. Jade was right next to him, basting while he turned. Nash loved how they did things together. He grabbed a bottle of water and made his way outside.

To his left, Ridge, Arlo and the Perry triplets' significant others—West, Asa and Camden—were playing football. Ridge cupped his hands and called out. "Get over here! We need a third person."

Shrugging off the doldrums, Nash jogged over to them. "What am I playing?"

"You're on defense," Arlo said.

"We're three-two," Ridge added. "So bring your A game."

West gripped the football and stepped forward. After

swinging the ball in an arc high above his head, he released it. Arlo jumped and snatched the ball midair before he sprinted down the field with Nash on his heels. Seeing his cousins run toward him, he braced for impact. That's when his eyes met those of the person standing by the sidelines. He froze for a beat before lifting his hand in a wave.

The next thing he felt was a *whoosh* and he was falling to the earth with a thud.

Chapter Twenty-Four

Earlier that day

"Honey, as much as I've loved having you here, you've got to get back to your life," Abena said, rocking Colt in her arms. He had been fussy the past few days, crying nonstop. After Nash's brash words, Imani had given the movers her parents' address since her penthouse was occupied—and she had needed her mother's comfort. "This little guy misses his daddy," her mother continued. She raised an eyebrow and settled farther into the couch of her living room. "And I'd bet all the shoes in my closet, he's not the only one."

It was a little past eight thirty in the morning and Abena had been up from dawn preparing her annual Thanksgiving breakfast feast. Because Jonathan and her father lived in a different time zone, Abena had started celebrating Thanksgiving at nine o'clock, which would be 6:00 p.m. in Dubai. Her grandparents, aunts and cousins were due to arrive in a few minutes and then the family would have a video conference while they shared their meals.

"I'm just giving Nash what he said he wanted." She jutted her chin and folded her arms.

"Yes, but at your heart's expense."

Imani snorted. "My heart is just fine." She looked away

from her mother's knowing stare and dabbed at her eyes. "Or it will be." Once she had arrived on her mother's door-step and had had a good cry, Imani had set up in her old bedroom of her parents' six-bedroom home, using the con-necting room for Colt's nursery. Most of her possessions were still in boxes. "I got over Nash before, I will again."

"I'll believe that when you stop checking your cell-phone notifications."

"Oh…you caught that?" Imani's cheeks warmed.

Her mother chuckled. "Yes. You've checked your phone at least ten times already this morning." She smoothed a hand down her burnt orange slacks, which she had paired with a cream sweater and nude pumps.

"I read online to avoid communication with your part-ner for at least seventy-two hours when you're upset about something. That way both parties have time to calm down and reflect on what they have done."

"Oh? How's that working out for you?" Her mother stood to place Colt in his bassinet. Imani was relieved to see he had finally fallen asleep. She followed her mother into the kitchen, and they began to place the food on the well-dressed table. Her mother had outdone herself with a spread of chicken, waffles, eggs, turkey bacon, a fruit-and-charcuterie board, cinnamon rolls and various Danishes and croissants. Everything was covered or wrapped in cel-lophane for when the rest of the family arrived.

"It's been tough," Imani admitted and exhaled. "He's texted and called but what else is there to say?" She shrugged. "He doesn't want to be a father to Colt."

"Doesn't *want* to be? Or doesn't think he can be?" Her mother wagged a finger. "Because there's a difference." Her gentle words pierced Imani's resolve.

She outstretched her hands. "I've tried to reassure him,

but it's like Nash doesn't get that there is no perfect parent. He doesn't understand that we just want him in our lives."

"And you're conveying that want by being away from him?" Abena pulled out a chair and sat, tapping the space next to her.

"Ah, er..." Imani twisted her lips and slid into the adjacent chair. "He believes Colt will be better off without him."

"And you believe differently, correct?"

"Yes, of course, I do. I know with all my heart that Nash will be the best father. The father that Colt needs. I've seen him in action and don't doubt it one bit."

"So why aren't you acting on that belief?"

Imani shook her head. "I don't get what you're asking."

"Nash is acting on his belief that he's no good for Colt by pushing you both out of his life. If you don't agree, why aren't you pushing back?"

"You expect me to chase after someone who told me that he was willing to take the chance that his son might want to have nothing to do with him if he's out of his life?" Her voice held an edge. Ooh, every time she thought about those words, ire curdled in her chest.

"I expect you to fight for what you believe and want. Fight for the man you love. And fighting isn't running back home to me, though I love having you."

Is that what she was doing? *Running?*

"My dear daughter, I love you, but you need staying power. When things get rough or you feel cornered, you run. How do you think I've stayed married to your father this long? Though we live thousands of miles apart, our bond is tight. That's because I refused to let distance interfere with our love and our commitment to each other."

"I didn't run..." A visual image of her racing off in her wedding gown from the courthouse and yet another of the moving truck and her SUV packed with her belongings as she evacuated Nash's guesthouse hit her mind. She drew in a breath. "Do I?"

"You do." Abena patted her hand. "You want a man who is honest with you. One who will tell you his deepest fears, knowing you will still be there, that you will have his back." Her mother cleared her throat. "When your father first left for Dubai, I was furious."

Imani gasped. "You were?"

"*Ab-sol-ute-ly* livid." Abena nodded. "He left me here with a brand-new baby so he could expand the family oil business. Can you imagine? I didn't speak to him for two weeks. But then one day, I heard about some explosion or something near where he worked and lived in Dubai and I was sick to my stomach. For days, I waited for word. But nothing. I couldn't take it no more. Though I'm not fond of flying, I left you with your grandparents and headed to Dubai."

"You did?" Imani's eyes were wide.

"You were too young to remember." Abena waved a hand. "When I got there, I headed straight to the hospital, my heart in my throat. All I could think of was, was Phillip gone? Did he die before I got to tell him how much I loved him?"

"Oh, my goodness." Imani's eyes misted. "Was he hurt?"

"No. He was helping. When I got there, I saw him covered in dirt and refuse but he had been helping to pull others to safety." Her mom shook her head. "I wanted to rage and hurl, but at that moment when our eyes connected, I knew what he needed. What *I* needed." She spread her arms wide. "I opened my arms and welcomed him."

Imani sniffled. "Wow…"

"I learned that day that love is more powerful than

anger." Abena's voice wobbled but she winked. "I'm pretty sure your brother was conceived that night."

"It's no wonder Jonathan loves Dubai." Imani laughed.

Abena joined in before she gave her daughter's hand a squeeze. "You have to decide for yourself if your love is more powerful than your anger at Nash. 'Cause I know this isn't about waiting seventy-two hours to communicate. You are mad at him for not choosing right, but how long do you plan on making him pay?"

That question stayed with Imani throughout their breakfast. While she enjoyed herself, she knew it was time to go back to her own family. It was time to return to Nash.

"Nash! Nash! Are you okay?"

Imani broke into a run toward the figure prostrate on the ground. She had dressed in a green blouse, dark blue jeans and brown cowboy boots, which was not exactly the best outfit for running. His family surrounded him while he lay still. Imani stood close behind them, her heart pounding in her chest. Her mother's story from that morning about almost losing her father echoed in her head. *This is different. He's okay.*

Ridge and Arlo pulled Nash to his feet. Holding his head, Nash grunted and rubbed his scalp. "I'm alright. I lost focus. For a second, I thought I saw Imani and..."

She stepped up, fiddling with one of the turkey earrings in her ear. "I'm right here."

His eyes went wide. "Imani? I thought you were back in Cactus Grove." His family dispersed, giving him pats on the back, along with some good ribbing blended with relief.

"I was. Your mom had invited me earlier in the week." She pointed at Wendy, who was holding Colt. Nash reached for her hand. The instant electricity flowed between them.

"I had Thanksgiving breakfast with family and then I drove out here to be with *my* family." She gave him a pointed stare while her words sunk in.

Nash touched his chest. "I'm glad you came." His eyes welled. "I've missed you and Colt more than I imagined I could."

Her chest tightened. "We've missed you, too." Wendy called out that it was time for them to gather at the table to eat. There was quite a spread—turkey, roast beef, barbecue chicken, corn, mashed potatoes, mac and cheese, green bean casserole, grilled asparagus, cheesecake and pies. Everything looked and smelled delicious. Since she hadn't eaten since breakfast, Imani was more than ready to enjoy their meal.

"We'll talk later?" Nash asked, linking his fingers with hers. She nodded and then he touched her face, as if reassuring himself that she was there. They took the last two chairs near the edge of the tent. Wendy came over with Colt in her arms.

Nash's face lit up. Imani could see the love reflected there and she silently thanked her mother for urging her to return. Nash held his son close to his chest and closed his eyes. "I love you, son. Daddy loves you." Then he kissed the top of Colt's head, not caring that they had an audience.

Imani would have fallen apart if Wendy hadn't cracked a joke—not that Imani heard what she said—but she laughed along with everyone, her heart suddenly joyous. Throughout the meal, Nash couldn't keep his hands off her. At one point, he drew her onto his lap, having handed off Cole to one of his cousins. Then he kissed her neck, her ears, her chin and, finally, her lips.

"Come up for air, man," Arlo called out. "You're ruining our appetites."

"Dang, you two need to give us a break with all the PDA," Ridge said.

Imani knew her face had to be beet red, but she didn't care. She was right where she needed to be. In Nash's arms. But she did have to answer nature's call. She gave him a peck on the lips. "I've got to use the bathroom. I'll be back in a jiffy."

Cupping her face with his hands, Nash pinned her with a fiery glance. "I love you and I am never letting you out of my sight again."

"I love you, too, but I won't be but a minute or two," Imani said, sliding off his lap.

"I'll come with you." Nash stood. "We'll be right back." He led her into the main house, ignoring the catcalls behind them. He showed her to the bathroom, waiting outside the door. As soon as she was finished, Nash snatched her into one of the empty bedrooms and closed the door.

"You know your family thinks we are up to no good in here," she giggled. Her heart was so happy for her to care too much.

"And they would be right." Nash plopped onto the bed, drawing her close. Resting his head against her abdomen, he exhaled. "I'm so glad you're back. I thought I had lost you and Colt for good."

"No. We just needed some thinking time." Imani tucked her index finger under his chin and prodded him to meet her eyes. "Our time apart showed me that there's nowhere else I'd rather be than here with you."

Nash pulled her down on the bed next to him. "I wish I could show how much I've missed you," he growled in her ear, then tugged on her earlobe with his teeth.

"We will have years for you to show me how much, but you can start later tonight," she said, caressing his cheek.

"Tonight?" he breathed out.

"Yes, the doctor said I'm good to go on the four week mark."

He grinned. "Well, Happy Thanksgiving to me."

"Happy Thanksgiving," she chuckled, fussing with his hair. "Did I tell you how much I love you?"

"Yes, but you can tell me again because I'll never tire of hearing it. And I'll never tire of telling you and Colt how much you mean to me."

"I love you, Nash Fortune. One lifetime will never be enough for me to show you how much." She drew his head down for a kiss.

Several minutes later, Imani and Nash rejoined the festivities outside. He beelined for his son, strapping the carrier to his chest. Everywhere he went, Colt was with him. Imani's heart rejoiced. Everything was finally as it should be.

It was late that night when Imani returned with Nash to his home. She trailed behind him up the stairs and followed him to the nursery. She gasped. It was the exact replica of the nursery in the guesthouse. She scanned the space. Her eyes met Nash's. "When did you do this?"

"While you were gone, I had time on my hands." He gave her a sheepish smile. "I was afraid to hope but I had to prepare for the possibility."

Fighting back tears, Imani said, "You do want Colt. You wouldn't have done this if you didn't."

"I do. I really do. I'm sorry it took you leaving for me to really see how much I want him in my life."

She wiped her face. "Colt is lucky to have you."

"And I'm blessed to have you both in my life. I'll never forget just how much."

They tiptoed inside the room, and rested Colt inside his crib. The baby squirmed then settled, his bottom in the air. Both parents released sighs of relief. Taking the baby monitor, Nash clasped her hand with his and led her down the hall to his master suite.

Another gasp escaped.

Done in whites and browns with huge windows providing a view of the lake, Imani lost her breath at the luxury of the furnishings and the pictures of her and Colt on the wall space. His painting from their night together was also on display. But, um, that bed was huge.

"You're the only woman to enter this space," Nash declared. "Well, except for my mother, when I just moved."

"Am I really?"

"Yes." Nash swung her in his arms. "You don't know how many nights I wish you were here with me." He placed her in the center of the bed. "No other woman has been in this bed, either."

"Good, because I plan to be the *only* one." She slipped out of her clothes, giving him a view of the lingerie she had worn underneath.

"Whoa. I'm so glad you got the all clear because there's no way I could lay beside you and not touch you when you're dressed like that," he groaned. "I'm going to make love to you all night so I hope you're up to the task."

"Well, I'm not one to back down from a challenge," she teased, her voice husky.

Nash went over to the chest on the other side of the room and took out a small box. Imani propped herself up on her arms, her mouth agape. "Is that what I think it is?" she squeaked out. Her heart started to pound in her chest.

His response was to slip to his knees. He wrapped his arms around her ankles and pulled her down to the edge of the bed. She sat up. When he opened the box, her breath caught at the solitaire sparkling in the moonlight. *Ohmy-*

goodness. Ohmygoodness. Her chest rose and fell. Was he about to do what she thought he was about to do?

He looked into his eyes. "Imani Porter, you have given me my son, the best gift of my life. Being without you these past days showed me I never want to wake up another morning without you at my side. I want to spend each sunset with you. I want to—"

She grabbed his head and kissed him to stop him from delivering the long speech. "Nash Fortune, can you skip ahead to the part where you ask me to marry you?" she asked. "We have love and the baby carriage, so let's get to it, shall we?"

He chuckled. "Alright. Imani Porter, will you agree to a name change and be mine for life?"

"Yes. Yes. A thousand yeses!" she exclaimed, holding out her hand, squirming with excitement.

Nash slid the ring on her finger. "A perfect fit."

She gave him a knowing grin. "Exactly." Nash stood her and drew her into his arms to seal their engagement with a searing kiss.

And now, everything was as it should be.

Finally.

* * * * *

HARLEQUIN
Reader Service

Enjoyed your book?

Try the perfect subscription for Romance readers and get more great books like this delivered right to your door.

See why over 10+ million readers have tried Harlequin Reader Service.

Start with a Free Welcome Collection with free books and a gift—valued over $20.

Choose any series in print or ebook. See website for details and order today:

   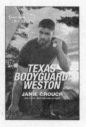

TryReaderService.com/subscriptions